ROGUE ANGEL

A Novel of Fra Lippo Lippi

by

Carol Damioli

DANTE UNIVERSITY OF
AMERICA PRESS

Library of Congress Cataloging-in-Publication Data

Damioli, Carol.
     Rogue angel : a novel of Fra Lippo Lippi / by Carol
Damioli.
          p. cm.
     ISBN 0-937832-33-2
     1. Lippi, Filippo, ca. 1406-1469--Fiction.
     2. Painters--Italy--Fiction.
      I. Title.
     PS3554.A487R64 1994
     813'.54--dc20   94-2676
                                         CIP

Dante University of America Press
17 Station Street
Box 843 Brookline Village
Boston, MA 02147

Contents

TO BRIAN
for not letting me quit

(Acknowledgments)

Excerpt from "Night of Stars" by Luis de Leòn, from *Luis de León; A Study of The Spanish Renaissance* by Aubrey FitzGerald Bell, 1925, reprinted by permission of Oxford University Press.

Excerpt from *Lives of the Artists* by Giorgio Vasari, translated and selected by George Bull, Penguin Classics, 1965, Harmondsworth, Middlesex, England, p. 132, Copyright © George Bull, 1965, reproduced by permission of Penguin Books Ltd.

Excerpt from Dante's "Paradiso", Canto XVII, 85-87, translated by P. H. Wicksteed, by permission of J. M. Dent, publisher.

Quote by Matteo Palmieri, from "Studies in Education during the Age of the Renaissance," by W. H. Woodward, 1906, p. 67, © Copyright Cambridge University Press.

Excerpt from "A Carnival Song" by Lorenzo de' Medici, reprinted by permission of the publishers from *A History of Italian Literature* by Ernest Hatch Wilkins, Cambridge, Mass.: Harvard University Press, © Copyright 1954, 1974 by the President and Fellows of Harvard College.

Excerpt from "Poor Loving Soul" by Louise Labé, from *Poems in Classical Prosody* by Robert Bridges, 1925, reprinted by permission of Oxford University Press.

Quote by Giovanni Boccaccio, from *THE PORTABLE RENAISSANCE READER*, edited by James B. Ross and Mary Martin McLaughlin. © Copyright 1953,

Chapter 1

You should not take a fellow eight years old
And make him swear to never kiss the girls.
                    Robert Browning, *Fra Lippo Lippi*

The stomp of an angry man's boots, and a boy's protesting whine echoed up the stairwell of Monna Lapaccia's tenement house.

Pazienza! she told herself. She took her customary place at the door and opened it at just the right moment. She watched calmly as one of Florence's civil guards shoved a struggling eight-year-old boy into the room.

"Here he is, Monna Lapaccia, caught stealing from the fruit vendor again. This really can't go on much longer," the guard said.

"Thanks for bringing my nephew home," Monna Lapaccia said, and shut the door. She eased her angular body into a chair at the rough-hewn table in the center of the room.

"Again, Lippo?" she said to the child. He stared back at his aunt in silent defiance, absently jabbing his left index finger toward the floor. Once Monna Lapaccia would have roared with rage, and shaken the boy like a rag doll. Now she just sighed with weary despair.

"He's right, you know. This really can't go on much longer. I'm an old woman," she said.

The boy backed away from her. "It was just one lousy little melon!" he said. "Nothing would have happened if--."

"Never mind. I've tried, Lippo, but I can't raise you. Tomorrow I'm taking you to the Carmelites," Monna Lapaccia said.

"No!" the boy screamed, shaking his chestnut hair. "I'll never go in there! When I climb the orchard fence and look down into that place, I see the monks walking around all day in those silly robes, dumb as donkeys! Or else they're mumbling some strange gibberish. I might as well move into the graveyard!" He was panting from excitement and the effort of putting his fear into words.

Monna Lapaccia quickly crossed herself against her nephew's blasphemy. "That strange gibberish is prayer to almighty God--something you could use a lot more of!"

"Why can't you just leave me alone?"

"Alone? And how would you live, alone on the streets? By stealing? I won't insult my brother's memory by letting his son become a thief. Be glad the Carmelites are willing to take in a boy like you! May God have mercy on them!"

The boy ran from the room and back down the stairs, back to the streets that would not sustain him.

Monna Lapaccia sighed and rubbed the painful spot in her back. She looked around the dim room, with its smelly oil lamps and straw mattresses. The boy's mother had died shortly after his birth, and Monna Lapaccia remembered the night two years later when her poor brother Tommaso also died. She had promised him that she would raise his son Filippo, called Lippo.

Now it was 1414, and the boy had given Monna Lapaccia an exasperating six years. She was thoroughly tired of the fights, the complaints from neighbors and the law, the ineffectiveness of punishment. In her declining health, the energetic Lippo was a force she could not handle.

As she sliced some bread for their evening meal, Monna Lapaccia heard the tolling of the bell at the Carmelite church. She realized that sending a boy like Lippo to a monastery was like sending an angry bull to solemn vespers. Still, she believed that the Carmelites would give him a good education, and the discipline he needed.

But the pain and guilt remained. After all, Lippo was family, and she had promised Tommaso.

As the unhappy pair walked down the Via dell'Ardiglione the next morning, Lippo, a scowl twisting his young face, vaguely considered running away. But to where? His aunt was right about the life of the streets-- the thieving, the hunger, the fights. If nothing else at least the Carmelites would give him a bed and food, however meager. Still he felt it was the end of the world, the end of all play and sunlight. Once more he was being abandoned--first by his mother, then his father, and now his Aunt Lapaccia, who had never really wanted him at all.

As they turned left onto Via Santa Monaca, Monna Lapaccia ached with a sense of failure, even as she told herself she could not do otherwise. Again she heard the tolling church bell, but now it seemed to pronounce judgment: *guilty, guilty!*

Neither had much time to brood. At the west end of Via Santa Monaca they entered the Piazza del Carmine, where, on the left, the red stone facade of the Church of Santa Maria del Carmine--St. Mary of the Carmelites--dominated the piazza. The sight of it gave Monna Lapaccia comfort, and filled Lippo with dread.

Just beyond the church stood the gray stone bulk of the monastery. The wooden door loomed twice Lippo's height. A boy not much older than Lippo answered Monna Lapaccia's knock, and ushered them into the office of Frate Jacopo di Alberto, the prior of the monastery.

"Frate Jacopo, this is my nephew, Filippo di Tommaso Lippi, who I've told you about," Monna Lapaccia said. She had often asked Frate Jacopo for advice as she struggled with Lippo. The prior was not surprised to see her bring the boy to the monastery.

Lippo eyed the monk suspiciously. *So you're the one behind all this*, he thought, but even he could find no malice in Frate Jacopo's face.

"I do hope this is right," Monna Lapaccia said. Frate Jacopo took her bony hand in his fat ones.

"Monna Lapaccia, you have been very loving and generous with the boy. You need not reproach yourself. God be with you," the prior said.

Monna Lapaccia turned to Lippo. Leaning down, she gave him a brief, tight hug. Then she hurried from the monastery.

"Forgive me, Tommaso," she said softly as she crossed the piazza.

Lippo felt monastic life seep so deeply into his unwilling being that soon he believed his body could lead him through the daily routine without conscious thought.

He rose with the monks and novices at dawn and went into the church for morning Mass. He stayed in the church a short time for silent meditation before a breakfast of bread and thin soup. Then he and the other novices cooked or laundered or swept or scrubbed, while the monks went to the chapter house for instruction and to openly confess their sins.

Then he went to classes, ate a late-afternoon meal, sat through more classes and did more chores. At sunset he gathered with the others for soup and group prayers, then bed. Meals were taken at long tables in the high-ceiling refectory. A monk read Scripture out loud during each meal, something Lippo found especially irritating. *Here, even our stomachs are lectured*, he lamented.

Yet Lippo noticed cracks in the façade of discipline. The scent from the kitchen sometimes betrayed the roasting of forbidden meat. Passing other monks' cells, he heard conversation--a violation of silence and solitude. And in the night, footsteps in the hall and on the stairs, then the opening and closing of the street door.

His classes made him squirm and daydream. He barely learned to read, regarding it as a waste of time. His writing remained rudimentary and ungrammatical, his arithmetic basic. He especially disliked the theological studies he had to make in preparation for taking monk's vows.

Lippo and the other novices slept 100 to a room, and prayed, ate and studied together. But the others approached their studies with a seriousness bordering on the grim, and he suspected they looked down on him, the orphaned son of a butcher.

He refused to plod obediently through the joyless dance, the numbingly predictable flow of days and months. Almost daily the monks reported to Frate Jacopo a list of Lippo's crimes:

> "He slept in the church during silent prayer--and snored!
> "He stole altar wine from the sacristy.
> "I caught him urinating in the cloister fountain."

When confronted by Frate Jacopo, Lippo denied all wrongdoing.

Each transgression earned Lippo hours in the church, alone on his knees, assigned to say the rosary. But the beads remained untouched in the folds of his robe while he studied the frescoes painted on the church's walls.

Lippo saw a true parade of piety--the Virgin, St. Anne, Carmelite saints, the Baptist, St. Stephen, St. Catherine, St. Sebastian, the Evangelists. He felt drawn especially to the works of Giotto di Bondone, with their well proportioned compositions and rich colors.

In the apse, Agnolo Gaddi, taught by Giotto's pupils, had painted scenes from the life of the Virgin. And on other walls Lippo saw more recent works, still influenced by Giotto: those of Gherardo Starnina and Spinello Aretino. All were inferior to that master, but still intriguing.

As intended, the scenes told Lippo stories of miracles, heroism, martyrdom and devotion. But he found himself looking more closely at the forms, the figures, the details of faces, the colors and lines. He wondered, casually, what it would be like to create such painted drama.

One day, during a lecture, a monk noticed Lippo busily scratching on a scrap of parchment with a piece of charcoal. When the monk saw that Lippo had made sketches, among them an unflattering likeness of the monk, he sent Lippo and the sketches to Frate Jacopo.

So once again Lippo stood before the prior. Frate Jacopo's patient, round placidity filled the bench behind his writing desk, and Lippo's unrepentant restless eyes searched the whitewashed office as if to find a means of escape. It was an often played scene, and each knew his part. Lippo waited to hear Frate Jacopo's usual chastising speech about the sinfulness of certain behavior, and about the chance for an education that Lippo was tossing away. He prepared to lie if accused of anything.

But this time, Frate Jacopo sat silently for several moments. He began to understand Monna Lapaccia's despair of ever reforming the boy. He bowed his head over his desk to ask God for patience. As he did, his eyes fell on Lippo's sketches.

The prior, though no expert, liked the detail in the drawing of the monk, and its small touch of whimsy.

"Lippo, this sketching--do you do this often?"

"Almost never, Frate," a startled Lippo said, anxious to say nothing that would worsen the inevitable punishment.

But Frate Jacopo simply nodded and looked at the sketches again before speaking.

"I know of several monks in Florence who are skilled painters. None of them belong to our monastery, but I may be able to have someone come here and tutor you in drawing," he said.

Lippo hardly paused. "Yes, I'd like that!" he said, showing enthusiasm for something for the first time since he had entered the monastery.

Lorenzo Monaco of Siena was a member of the Camaldolite monastery of Santa Maria degli Angeli in Florence. For years he had lived outside the cloister on the income from his paintings, and illustrations for sacred manuscripts. He was engaged to come several hours a week to the Carmelite monastery to tutor Lippo.

"I want to learn everything about drawing that there is to know. And the same for painting," Lippo told Fra Lorenzo.

"That's a lot to learn. Let's just take things a step at a time," Fra Lorenzo replied. None of his previous students had shown Lippo's promise and spirit. From Fra Lorenzo, Lippo absorbed the direction and encouragement he needed, while the monk, after a life of modesty and self denial, dared to bask in Lippo's esteem.

"Today we'll work on your pen and ink technique," Fra Lorenzo said.

"But I'd rather draw with charcoal or chalk, Fra Lorenzo--they show the shapes of things better, and the effects are more, oh, I don't know, mysterious..."

"Perhaps 'atmospheric' is what you mean."

"...Yes, at-mos-pheric, and they're soft and easy to use, so I can draw faster and easier. Charcoal and chalk let me set down much quicker what I see," Lippo said.

Fra Lorenzo tried not to dampen Lippo's eagerness. "You're right about the qualities of charcoal and chalk, but you need practice with pen and ink. It teaches you to shape contours precisely and to create

clear detail," the monk insisted. Reluctantly Lippo
picked up a sharpened quill, dipped it in ink, and began
to draw on a sheet of parchment.

"Now draw this lemon again, this time from this
angle," Fra Lorenzo said, positioning the fruit on a desk.
Watch the contours--that's it." Lippo continued until he
had covered an entire sheet of parchment with lemons,
each from a slightly different angle. Suddenly he set
down his pen.

"What is it like to live outside the monastery, Fra
Lorenzo?" he asked.

"I live quite simply, the same as any monk. I still
attend Mass every day, and take time for private prayer.
I make contracts for my work and fulfill them, and that's
about all, except for these sessions with you, of course."

"But living outside, you must know more about
the world than other monks," Lippo said slowly, savoring
the thought. "There must be something special out
there--something better than the grimy streets I grew up
in."

"Lippo, nothing out there distracts me from my
vows, or my work," Fra Lorenzo said. The dreamy look
on Lippo's face troubled him, and his usually soft voice
grew firm. "Besides, it can be ugly and brutish out
there--not like this house of holy men. Still, my living
outside the monastery is a special privilege, for which I
daily thank God. It is something given to few, Lippo--I
must warn you, don't get any foolish or unholy ideas!"

"No, of course I won't," Lippo said, but the
dreamy look remained. "I was just wondering."

The lesson continued as before, yet both sensed
vaguely that nothing was quite the same. Something had
shifted there amid the parchment and the ink, a force
weighty and incomprehensible as the will of God.

The hours with Fra Lorenzo were the only hours when Lippo felt alive and happy. His pranks and mischief declined as he spent his time drawing everyone in sight--the prior, the sacristan, the other novices. He drew the murderer who took sanctuary at the altar, and the grimaces and gestures of his accuser. Peasant women and their babies served as his models of the Madonna and her Child.

He no longer snored in the church, but imagined the figures he might one day paint on its walls, alongside the Giottos and others he had admired so often. Finally Lippo had found something in which he could excel, and Frate Jacopo and the other monks offered prayers of thanks.

While the monks rejoiced in Lippo's changed behavior, there was no one to help him through other, less evident changes. No other monk could know about the muscling of his chest or the firming of his calves and thighs beneath his novice's habit. And no monk realized that the confused yearnings of youth had begun to torment him. Occasionally in the darkness of the novice's dormitory Lippo calmed the inner clamor with his own hands, but it always returned. He never confessed this wicked act.

"Young Lippo learns quickly," Fra Lorenzo told Frate Jacopo one day. "Now that he has a thorough grounding in drawing, it's time he learned how to paint. Let him come for a few hours a week to my studio in Via San Giovanni. It's only a few steps from here."

Frate Jacopo chuckled. "I'm afraid you don't know Lippo. His aunt brought him here because she couldn't control him, and to let him leave here, however briefly, while he's still so young--well, it could present him with temptations he's not able to fight," he said.

"But there's something in Lippo's drawings that I didn't teach him," Fra Lorenzo countered. "He is no mere craftsman, no imitator. What he has can only be a gift from God. Perhaps it's unforgivably bold of me, Frate, but I must say it. To let this gift remain unborn behind these walls would be shameful. If you let him come to my studio, I will take responsibility for his behavior," he said.

A troubled look came over Frate Jacopo's face.

"The monastic life is slowly crumbling, Fra Lorenzo. I have to struggle to see that fasts and abstinence are observed. Our rules of silence and solitude are not respected. And there is no contrition for these sins! Soon it will lead to worse--I've heard, in some monasteries, of concubinage, of monks going to brothels... I'm helpless to stop it." Frate Jacopo sighed. "All right--Lippo may visit your studio. But I warn you--the boy's spiritual and moral life during the hours he's not here will be quite a burden. With Lippo you may need every one of the virtues that the Camaldolites have taught you."

Fra Lorenzo sat back in his chair, satisfied. "You know, Prior, given his talent and his restless nature, you may not be able to keep him here forever, anyway," he said.

The chance to visit an actual painter's studio, and to learn how to paint, thrilled Lippo. He knew he mustn't ruin the opportunity through childish misbehavior. But even on the short walk to Fra Lorenzo's studio each week, he managed to find temptation. He longed to join the boys playing dice games on the street. Often his hand itched to reach toward the fruit vendor's lemons, figs, or melons, just to see if he could still do it. And if a young maiden flashed him a teasing smile from an upstairs window, was it so wrong to smile back?

In 1421, when Lippo was 15, the day approached when he was to take his monk's vows. He went half-heartedly through the final preparations, constantly aware of longings inconsistent with a vow of celibacy. For Lippo, the taking of monk's vows was certainly not the culmination of a deeply felt calling. It was simply a step that had been implicit since the day Monna Lapaccia brought him to the monastery.

Just before the profession ceremony, Lippo, crossing the monastery cloister, caught sight of his reflection in the fountain. He stopped to take one long, last look at himself as a layman. He didn't care that such self-centered gazing would surely bring a reprimand, if any monk noticed him and happened to tell Frate Jacopo.

He wondered whether he would look different after taking his vows. Given a choice, he would be taller and more slender. He had the average height and stocky build of many Florentines--a body suited for long rides by mule over rough roads. His face was square and his forehead low over brown eyes, full lips and a blunt nose and chin. His ears stuck out a bit, and his brown hair bristled in the tonsure he'd been given several months before. He wanted to let his hair grow back, but in the monastery there was no escaping the regular ordeal of scissors and razor on one's scalp.

In the way that news often drifted over the monastery walls to the world outside, Monna Lapaccia heard about Lippo's profession, and felt relief and vindication. She'd heard occasional rumors about Lippo's behavior, but she reasoned that with the taking of his monk's vows, all that would surely stop. Perhaps in some way she had kept her promise to Tommaso after all.

Weeks later, encouraged by Frate Jacopo, Lippo also took priest's vows. "It will increase your devotion," the prior told him vaguely. He was afraid to tell Lippo his true motive, afraid it would put premature ideas in the young monk's head: as a priest, Lippo might get a sinecure from the bishop, allowing him to live outside the monastery and paint, free from worries about money.

A few months after taking his vows, Lippo and some other young Carmelites made a pilgrimage to the monastery of St. Francis, in ancient Fiesole, Florence's mother city on a hill to the northeast.

They set out in the chill of dawn. Only early fishermen on the Arno River saw them cross the Ponte alla Carraia. They breathed the damp stone smell of Florence as they crossed piazzas and passed churches, tenements and palazzi, some bearing corner shrines or sacred images painted on their doorways. The young monks didn't speak, and heard only the slap of their own sandals on the city's gray streets.

Through Florence's walls they emerged into the late-summer countryside. Florentine merchants, while in Southampton or the Algarve, dreamed of this land: the low rounded green hills, the sentinel cypresses, the gray trembling olive leaves. Streams wound through meadows full of wild flowers, soon to glow under the clear, sharp Tuscan sunlight.

The monks passed stone cottages, secluded villas behind plump hedges, tiny shrines where cart paths crossed.

Peasants hitched oxen to plows and began another day of wringing oil and wine and grain from the stony and sandy soil of the fields and vineyards, in much the same arduous way they had done for centuries.

At last the monks reached Fiesole.

Legend said it was built by Atlas, the Titan. Lippo had also heard that the Roman rebel Catiline took refuge there before leaving for his last battle, and death, 63 years before Christ's birth. Fiesole had been an Etruscan settlement, then a Roman commune.

The cathedral's elegant bell tower watched over the piazza, the nearby bishop's palazzo, and the town hall. The monks stopped to examine the wide view of the Arno Valley that swept away below them, a palette of green tints and the dots of stone dwellings. Florence looked like a silent, insignificant cluster huddled at the river: its daunting wall a mere red bootlace; its incomplete cathedral; its towers, normally so imposing, appeared from this vantage point like straight gray quills.

One final short slope crowning Fiesole brought the monks to the monastery of St. Francis, on the ruins of an old citadel. After praying all day with the monks there, the Carmelites headed back down the hill toward home.

They passed an olive grove. Lippo, surveying the lush scenery with an eye for subjects to draw, caught a distant glimpse of a girl close to his age. She seemed to vanish so quickly behind some trees that Lippo could not be sure she really existed. Perhaps she was a fairy or a forest nymph that his lustful mind had only imagined. But the tiny flash aroused him mightily and made him determined to find out.

"My brothers, this view of Florence is too beautiful to lose," he said to the other monks. "I'd like to stay on this hill long enough to try my hand at drawing it, before the daylight is gone." He pulled from his habit a scrap of parchment and a bit of charcoal that he carried everywhere.

The other monks had seen Lippo taken by sudden inspiration many times. If the girl really existed, they had not seen her, so none of them doubted Lippo's intention. They continued toward Florence without him.

Lippo sat on the ground and watched the departing monks as twilight began to fall. When the monks were well out of sight, he rose, turned around, and nearly ran into the girl, who stood so close and so unexpectedly behind him.

The Madonna of Humility, also known as the Trivulzio Madonna. The Carmelites of Florence commissioned this altarpiece, and hung it over the altar dedicated to St. Angelo in the church transept. At the right are the Carmelite saints Angelo and Albert, at the left is St. Anne.

Chapter 2

Here beauty infinite
Unveils itself, and light, quintessence pure,
Transparent gleams: no night
Its radiance may obscure,
Spring's flowered splendor here is ever sure.

Luis de León, *Night of Stars*,
trans. Aubrey FitzGerald Bell

Wordlessly, she looked Lippo over from his shaved head to his sandals. She looked into his eyes for a long moment and smiled. Lippo started to speak, but the girl turned and walked slowly toward a heavily wooded area nearby, glancing back at him once. *So you are real*, Lippo thought as he followed her. She was not the stuff of fantasy at all, but a girl of the soil, in peasant's skirt and apron, her hair veiled.

They entered the woods. When Lippo held her, and they kissed, he felt like a long-starved prisoner finally being fed. He pressed her closer to his awakened body, and slid her veil easily from her soft hair. He had never known such smoothness as her ample breasts and belly, or such fire as he found when she opened herself and he slipped inside her.

He found relief quickly. For several more minutes, Lippo and the girl laid very still together in the woods, as the twilight deepened and the trees melted into a curtain around them.

Then suddenly the girl stood up, straightened her skirt, and walked away casually, as if leaving the fields at the end of the day. She didn't look back.

Lippo looked down at his rumpled habit and his drawing tools scattered in the grass. He felt no shame. Instead a delightful buoyancy overcame him--something unknown in the heavy atmosphere of the monastery. He'd caught a suggestion of the feeling when engrossed in his drawing, but only a weak, pale version of what he felt now. *So now I've known Woman* he thought, as he continued down the hill toward Florence. He sighed long and deeply. The memory of that girl never left him, although he never saw her again, or knew her name.

At once the childish desires of dice games and stolen fruit fell away. Only one forbidden fruit attracted Lippo now, and he didn't try to resist. Lorenzo Monaco's ill health had brought an end to Lippo's lessons, but there were other exits from the monastery. If someone rushed there seeking a monk to give last rites to a dying relative, Lippo packed his prayer book and holy oil. If a widow sent a servant to the monastery with orders to bring back a monk to give her spiritual counsel, Lippo jumped to volunteer. He was the monk most willing to go to the goldsmith to order altar vessels, or to the tailor for new vestments.

He found widows both handy and eager. They had known pleasures of the flesh, and many had no intention of giving them up. As widows, they had more freedom than wives or maidens. They could send for Lippo at the monastery by name on some religious pretext, or meet him casually on the street during an evening stroll.

It was more difficult to arrange to be with a wife, and the penalties for adultery could be severe. On rare occasions they invited Lippo into their homes while their merchant husbands were away on long trips.

Servant girls had a few hours off each week--they could meet Lippo at the city gates for a brief excursion into the woods. But maidens were nearly impossible to bed. Their fathers kept them indoors after age 13, except to go to Mass, and then they were always veiled and escorted. For the special delights he could only get from women who lived to please men, Lippo occasionally visited one of Florence's civic brothels.

Lippo never forced himself on any unwilling woman. He considered men who did so more loathsome than maggots. His women had to be not only desirable but desirous; lovers who whispered a fervent yes! to his age-old question.

Slowly the young monk's reputation grew. Many monks, both Carmelites and others, had occasionally sought worldly pleasures, but Lippo's insatiability and brazen openness made him different. Some Florentines thought his behavior reprehensible; many shrugged it off. Monna Lapaccia shook her head in resignation. Others who had known Lippo in childhood were not at all surprised, and were smugly satisfied that he had turned out as they predicted.

Lippo's bold ways profoundly embarrassed the Carmelites. In desperation Frate Jacopo locked the door of Lippo's cell after the monk returned to it late one night. The next morning, when Lippo realized what had happened, he screamed with anger.

Frate Jacopo was ready. "Pray, Fra Filippo," the prior said from the corridor outside.

"Pray? Are you mad? All right, I'll give you prayers!" Lippo ripped open the shutters of his cell's tiny window, then grabbed a prayer book and tore out the pages. One by one he tossed them out the window, and they fluttered in the sunshine to the cloister below.

Monks passing through the cloister on their way to morning Mass stopped to watch the spectacle.

"And that's not all!" Lippo roared. The amused monks waited for a few moments. Then Lippo thrust a chamber pot out the window and emptied its contents onto the cloister's grass.

The confinement continued for twenty-four hours. Frate Jacopo repeated it every few months, but it had no effect on young Lippo's inclinations. The fox ran loose again each time. Some monks urged Frate Jacopo to expel Lippo from the monastery, but the prior always refused. He reasoned that even if a man chose to set himself far from God, it was not the right of other men to drive the offender from God's community. Still, the prior despaired of ever seeing a change of Lippo's heart or ways. *I'm helpless*, he thought, *just as I told Fra Lorenzo*.

Perhaps the wise Frate Jacopo understood that Lippo's forays outside the monastery were not made solely in search of willing female flesh. For Lippo, simply walking the streets of Florence was pure joy. Unlike most of the other monks, he had left the outside world unwillingly, and despite its miseries, he had missed it profoundly ever since.

Lippo's usual path took him across the Arno on Ponte alla Carraia, then through busy, narrow streets to the mercato, the bustling commercial center of town, where the Roman Forum had once stood.

There he watched the fruit and vegetable sellers by their booths, the drapers and the bakers. Barbers shaved people in the open. Tailors worked in doorways as servants and housewives gathered to buy cooked food. Here, the smell of fresh bread wafted by, there, Lippo caught the unmistakable smell of the fishmonger's stall. Bales of silk and barrels of grain sat ready for sale; furniture makers and goldsmiths showed off their work. Town criers called out, beggars wandered, children and gamblers rolled dice on the paving stones. Dogs, pigs, and geese ran everywhere. Vagabonds, nobles and hucksters all played their parts. People greeted and insulted each other and argued in rising and falling waves of the Tuscan language: musical enough for poetry, but with natural strength and firmness.

Lippo loved to search the faces of the Florentines--not only the women, but the men, both rich and poor; the old, the children. He stored away impressions of their matt complexions that ranged from deep honey to olive; their hair, usually dark, with eyes to match, often keenly intelligent and shrewd.

The curves and angles of their bodies, seldom tall and often husky, also fascinated Lippo. He noted the fine hand movements of the jewelers and tailors, and the stretch of the baker's arms as he shoveled bread dough into communal ovens.

From the market Lippo liked to stroll south onto Via Calimala, which led to the curious Orsanmichele, a squarish structure housing a communal granary on the second floor, and a delicate and ornate chapel for the city's craft workers below. On the street, silk merchants sold fabric in shops or under awnings, while money-changers dickered at their desks.

He stepped faster when he saw the fortress-like Palazzo Signoria, the seat of Florentine government, and named for the city's ruling body. Here officials wore fancy robes, ate lavish meals while musicians enter-tained, and used their positions, won in rigged elections, to favor friends and bully enemies. When not so occupied, they made peace and war, and levied taxes. For the privilege of this power, men fought in the streets, and exiled, assassinated, and destroyed each other generation after generation.

But Lippo ignored Florence's burial grounds, torture dens and prisons. Whether Florence shouted or murmured, its noise blended for him into a song of vitality, of liberty and delight. The song rang out in bold contrast to the solemnity of Santa Maria del Carmine, and Lippo needed to hear it as he needed the sun. It was the larger world he had dreamed he would one day know, beyond the monastery, beyond the pain of Via dell'Ardiglione. By walking in it, Lippo felt part of it, and ever less a part of the cloistered life.

He especially enjoyed the parts of the city where many painters and sculptors had their studios: Via Por Santa Maria, the streets behind the cathedral, or the Santa Croce quarter.

When Lorenzo Monaco died, Lippo's wanderings among these studios took on a more desperate intensity. He feared that without Fra Lorenzo he was direction-less, and his painting would stagnate. He needed more than ever to absorb various turns of technique, style, and composition from the masters. So Lippo moved avidly from one studio to another, his mind open and active.

Yet it was the most unlikely master of all, and in the most unlikely place, who would emerge from this creative fury and alter Lippo's life deeply and forever.

Lippo returned from a dalliance one day to find the monastery in an uproar. Wrapped in memories of pleasure, he paid little attention to the monks breaking the rule of silence as they hurried toward the cloister. Slowly he realized that something more compelling than the usual quiet contemplation must be taking place there.

"Have you seen him?"

"I think he's still in the cloister."

"He's big as an ox, they say--with manners to match!"

Lippo followed the other monks to the cloister, where all eyes were on a tall, broad-shouldered young man. He ignored the monks as he took careful measurements of the walls.

Lippo learned that this was the painter Tommaso di Ser Giovanni di Mone, known as Masaccio, a nickname that meant hulking or sloppy Tom. He had certainly earned it. Ill-fitting, paint-spattered clothes draped his body, and he let his hair take untidy flight.

At age 24, Masaccio had a modest reputation as an artist. He had done some paintings for the Carmelite church in Pisa, and painted a fresco representing the Trinity in Florence's church of Santa Maria Novella. His figures were monumental in their proportions, yet convincingly realistic, and he knew well the current theories on perspective. Other painters found Masaccio's powerful work exciting and bordering on the revolutionary, but many people spurned its lack of charm and conventional beauty. Some Carmelite monks in Pisa who appreciated painting had recommended Masaccio to their brothers in Florence. So when the time came for the Carmelite church of Florence to be consecrated by the archbishop, the two monks turned to Masaccio to paint a portrayal of the event on their cloister walls.

At once Lippo decided that Masaccio's arrival at the monastery was an omen, a chance to fill the gap Lorenzo Monaco had left.

He pushed through the crowd and planted himself directly in front of Masaccio. "I am Fra Filippo di Tommaso Lippi," he said. "Teach me to paint."

The Madonna of Corneto Tarquinia. The Archbishop of Florence, Giovanni Vitelleschi, commissioned this work. It shows the Madonna and Child in an intimate domestic setting.

Chapter 3

I painted, and my picture was like life;
I gave my figures movement, passion, soul;
They breathed. Thus, all others
Buonarotti taught; he learnt from me.
         Annibale Caro's epitaph for Masaccio

Masaccio looked at Lippo and smirked. *Yet another painter-monk!* He wondered if there were something in the meager food served at monasteries, or perhaps the water, that implanted in monks an urge to paint. He knew the work of Fra Lorenzo Monaco, and the paintings of the Dominican monk Fra Giovanni from Fiesole. But another painter-monk in Florence now? That was one too many.

He didn't mean to be rude. Masaccio was simply a man who paid as little attention to others as he did to himself. He had just one care in life, and that was his painting. But the intensity of Lippo's expression softened his response.

"Fra Filippo," Masaccio repeated, touching his scanty beard. "This is quite flattering, but there's not much you can learn about painting through the work I'm about to do here. This will be a simple monochrome, in shades of green and black. But I'll be coming back here soon to paint frescoes in the Brancacci chapel, and then maybe we'll see what I can teach you."

Lippo doubted Masaccio's claim that he could learn nothing from the work in the cloister, but he did not persist. Instead he spent much of the next several weeks silently watching Masaccio create his powerful figures--solid and full of grandeur and dignity, and as unadorned as the man himself. They occupied real space, instead of appearing suspended in thin air. They were so utterly different from the delicate, flat shapes of Lorenzo Monaco.

After Masaccio left, Lippo waited, often escaping the monotony of the monastery, concentrating on his drawing when he couldn't escape, and wondering if and when Masaccio would ever return.

After nearly a year Masaccio did return to the monastery. With him came the Florentine painter Masolino da Panicale, who had distinguished himself with the frescoes he'd painted in the church of San Clemente in Rome.

Lippo presented himself to Masaccio and reminded him of what the painter had said the day they met. Without waiting for a response, Lippo spread some of his drawings on the floor of the right transept chapel for the painter's inspection.

Masaccio prepared to say something mildly complimentary and get on with his work, certain that the drawings would be hopelessly inferior.

But the spark of promise in the drawings impressed him. "Well, if you've waited this long, you must be in earnest," he said. So, in his laconic style, Masaccio continued the instruction cut short by Lorenzo Monaco's death.

"Nature is my inspiration. Human figures should be natural, realistic and living," was his first counsel. "And light--light is everything! Note where it comes from, how it transforms figures and objects."

The Brancacci family's chapel, at the bottom of the church's right transept, was not large. About 20 people could kneel there together in prayer. The side walls rose two stories high, up to large lunettes and a vaulted ceiling. Light entered through a tall, narrow mullioned window in the rear wall. The wealthy Florentine silk merchant and ambassador Felice di Michele Brancacci hoped that sponsoring the chapel's decoration would link his family with the Carmelites, so dedicated to prayer and good works.

Brancacci hired the two painters, Masaccio and Masolino, and instructed them to depict in the frescoes certain scenes from the life of St. Peter. They composed the frescoes and worked on them together for several months. Then Masolino left for Hungary to work for a Florentine who held an important post there, leaving Masaccio to finish the job.

The fresco technique was a quick and economical way to decorate large, unbroken wall surfaces. But it was a demanding medium, requiring a dexterous and resolute hand, and sound judgment.

First, the wall surfaces needed preparation. Workers erected scaffolds with platforms large enough to accommodate the apprentices and all the equipment needed for the job--brushes, paint pots, buckets and other tools. Masaccio made sure the scaffolds were the right height and were placed correctly.

A thick, rough coat of plaster, called *arriccio*, was brushed onto the wall surface. It covered the rough stones and bricks of the wall and filled in the cracks between them, making the wall smooth and suitable for painting. Lippo learned how to control the consistency of the plaster and how to spread it on the wall smoothly, yet not so smooth that it lacked the roughness to hold yet another layer of plaster.

Masaccio then used plumb lines, a compass and a level to determine the center of the composition, and to find true horizontal and vertical.

He outlined the composition with charcoal on the dry plaster, showing the positions of objects in space and the details of figures and buildings.

Then Masaccio brushed a watery red paint over the lines of the charcoal drawing. The result was called a sinopia. After it dried, he brushed off the charcoal, leaving only a web of red lines. The apprentices would use the sinopia as a map to find their way around the fresco as they worked.

Finally the day arrived when paint was to be applied to the chapel walls. Lippo did not understand when Masaccio said to him that morning, with a mysterious smile, "Now you're going to see something."

In the fresco technique, the painter applied color to wet plaster, causing a permanent chemical bond between pigment and plaster. To begin, an apprentice applied a patch of new plaster to the wall. Because it was necessary to cover no more than could be completed in a single painting session, the size of the patch varied depending on the part of the composition it would contain. If a highly detailed face was to be painted, a small patch of plaster would be applied; but if the work centered on a large undetailed object, such as the sky or a barren hillside, then a much larger area could be plastered, because the painter could work more quickly.

"You see, Lippo, the patches must be painted not only while the plaster is still damp, but while it's at a certain degree of dampness, because dampness causes the pigments to dry to different shades. If I apply a brown pigment to a patch 10 minutes old, it will dry to quite a different shade than if I applied the same pigment to a patch half an hour old. So if a color runs across two or more patches, it's essential to paint both at the same stage of wetness," Masaccio said.

"Then a painter must be a master of timing and planning," Lippo said.

"Yes, and that's not easy, with the changes in humidity and temperature from hour to hour and day to day. If I miscalculate, the color of one object changes from patch to patch. And the only way to correct a mistake is by chipping out the plaster, and re-plastering."

"Why couldn't you just paint over the error after the wall has dried?" Lippo asked.

"Because the unbonded over paint would eventually fall off the wall," Masaccio said. "The dry air in this region makes this technique ideal. You won't see a lot of frescoes in Venice--it's too humid there."

The painting began. Lippo watched a frantic, noisy race to get the patches laid in and painted at just the right intervals. It seemed to him an enterprise almost comical in its fury, yet underlined with a certain degree of coordination and order. Masaccio painted the figures and other essential parts, and each apprentice, when not mixing or spreading plaster, painted less important and decorative elements.

Slowly the scenes unfolded. On the chapel's left wall, at the entrance, Adam and Eve depart from Eden in naked disgrace. Next to them, against a mountainous background, Jesus tells St. Peter how to pay the temple tax. Below, Masaccio began the scene in which Sts. Peter and Paul raise the dead son of Theophilus.

On the back wall, to the left of the altar, St. Peter heals the sick by letting his shadow fall on them as he walks by. On the same wall, to the right of the window, St. Peter baptizes shivering converts. Below that, the saint distributes alms, and Ananias lies dead at his feet.

Lippo's admiration for Masaccio grew as he watched the painter and the apprentices work amid trowels, buckets of plaster and water, and dishes of paint, sometimes high above the chapel floor. Lippo's mind, so dull in the lecture hall, devoured the fresco process and held the imprint of it as surely as the Brancacci chapel walls held Masaccio's colors.

Over several months Masaccio taught Lippo not only specific techniques, but the current theories of perspective, how to choose colors, and how to compose a picture. Masaccio endlessly impressed Lippo with the care he used in painting the human body--scrupulous observation of nature helped him create vigorous nudes, with realistic limbs. Lippo also admired Masaccio's use of shade and light to model figures and give them a third-dimensional reality. Masaccio was not interested in the gracefulness or refined elegance that dominated Florentine painting, but strove to paint expressive figures, appropriate to the tasks they performed. He was also a brilliant colorist. And Masaccio's perceptive eye led him to weave into the frescoes landscapes with trees, plants, hills and skies, which most previous painters had only treated symbolically. Felice Brancacci wanted painting of the highest order, and he got it, beyond imagining.

As Lippo studied and worked, he longed for words of approval from his master. His respect and enthusiasm touched Masaccio, but words emerged from the great painter rarely and awkwardly. Still, Lippo was so happy to have Masaccio's guidance that he even curtailed his pleasure-seeking forays outside the monastery--the highest compliment Lippo could possibly pay to the painter.

One morning, in 1428, the unfinished chapel was empty when Lippo arrived. He sought out Frate Jacopo, who said Masaccio had left the previous night for Rome.

Abandoned yet again! And without a word, Lippo thought. He wondered painfully whether the artist had been humoring him the whole time.

"Cardinal Branda Castiglione, of Lombardy, asked Masaccio to decorate a chapel in his titular church in Rome. I suppose when a cardinal calls, men like Brancacci have to wait their turn," the prior said.

"So Masaccio *had* to leave, then," Lippo said.

"Oh yes, our Masaccio had no choice. Don't feel abandoned, Fra Filippo! Before he left, he spoke highly of you," the prior said, to Lippo's great relief. "He said there's little more he can teach you. And if Masaccio says you're ready, that's good enough for me. There are some walls here in the monastery and church that need a painter's touch. Teach us through the sacred images you create."

Joy overwhelmed Lippo. He knew, finally, that he had managed to impress his master. And he suddenly realized how much kindness Frate Jacopo had shown him over the years. This man had given him a home, put up with endless childish pranks, and refused to cast him out despite outrageously sinful behavior. Now Frate Jacopo was entrusting the monastery's walls to Lippo's brushes. In a rare burst of gratitude and sensitivity, Lippo threw his arms around the old man and hugged him.

"Why, Frate? Why are you being so kind to me, much more than I deserve?"

"God sends all of us little tests of our patience. Perhaps you are one of mine."

Lippo plunged with mad enthusiasm and inspiration into plans for the church and monastery--sketching, measuring the walls, hiring assistants. Yet when it came time to apply paint to any surface, he was methodical, and his concentration profound. He painted a praiseworthy fresco depicting scenes from the life of St. John the Baptist. On a pilaster--a column set into the wall-- near the organ he did a painting of St. Marziale that everyone compared favorably with Masaccio's work. At last Lippo was master of the very walls that had once dominated and enclosed and threatened to suffocate him.

Soon the news reached the monastery that Masaccio had died in Rome of the plague. He was not yet 27 years old. The death saddened all Florence's artists, and those patrons who could appreciate Masaccio's brilliance. The architect Filippo Brunelleschi called it a terrible loss. In his grief Lippo felt inadequate and exposed. *I have lost another master.* Some said he had come to understand his teacher's style so well that Masaccio's spirit must have entered Lippo's body. Lippo found such comments excessive.

His work improved steadily. In 1430, the year of Lippo's 24th birthday, the clerk of the monastery wrote "Painter" after Lippo's name in the monastery record.

In the cloister, Lippo painted his first major work--a large fresco showing scenes from the history of the Carmelite order. It occupied a special place of honor, next to Masaccio's Consecration.

The Carmelites commissioned his first large panel picture in tempera on wood. It would depict the Madonna and Child, surrounded by child-angels and three saints. First Lippo visited a carpenter to order the panel, made from seasoned poplar boards. To make the wooden surface clean, dry and smooth required great care.

"First, sand the wood. Then mix up some sawdust and glue, and fill those knot holes with it. Then sand the whole thing smooth again," Lippo instructed his helpers as they gathered around the work table.

The next step was to coat the area to be painted with size, a pasty liquid made from boiled sheep parchment. A thin coat of size was first applied with a large bristle brush and allowed to dry. Then came at least two more coats of a thicker, stronger size, sealing the wood and making a smooth, stable surface for additional layers.

Lippo showed his helpers how to tear up strips of linen and glue them to the panel, forming yet another layer between the wood and the final paint surface.

"Why must we do all this layering, Fra Filippo?" one of the younger helpers asked.

"Because wood is porous and unstable. It shrinks and grows as the temperature and humidity change. If we applied paint directly to the wood, it would crack and flake with the movement of the panel. So all this fuss and bother is to protect the paint from the wood's movement, and to keep the wood's moisture out of the paint," Lippo replied.

The final basic layers were gesso--a thin mixture of plaster, glue and water. The helpers applied several coats of gesso to make the surface even. These were allowed to dry for several days, then scraped and sanded smooth.

"Now make the gesso extremely fine, slick, and thinner," Lippo said. "Then, do this." He rubbed some of the new batch of gesso on the panel by hand. His helpers applied eight additional layers, each before the previous one had dried.

After the panel had dried thoroughly in the sun, the helpers spent hours scraping the dry gesso until it was almost as sleek as ivory, making it an even, absorbent surface that would readily take the paint.

At last it was time for Lippo to put his personal stamp on the work by applying the underdrawing. At the request of the Carmelites, Lippo surrounded the Madonna and Child with childlike angels, St. Anne, and two Carmelite saints--Sts. Angelo and Albert. The piece would be wide enough to top a broad altar, and the composition would be roughly triangular, accentuating the Virgin by coming to a point above her head. To focus attention on the figures, the background would be a pale bluish gray, instead of the traditional gold.

With charcoal, Lippo outlined the figures, then gave them substance and form by putting in the light and dark shading. Lippo worked without preparatory drawings, but composed as he went along, experimenting and refining for several days. He used a feather to erase a mistake or an unsatisfactory line.

When he was satisfied, the helpers brushed off the charcoal drawing with a feather until only a trace remained on the panel. Then Lippo reinforced the outlines with a small, sharp miniver bristle brush and a watery ink. The remaining charcoal was brushed away, to keep it from marring and discoloring the paint.

The next step was preparation of the paints. One by one, the smells of the various pigments filled the room as Lippo's helpers ground them into powders: minerals, berries, flowers, metal oxides, even insects, and a dozen other materials.

Dark red came from the madder plant, crimson from the root of a plant from the Arabian peninsula, purplish red by grinding certain sea shells. The dried roots of an aquatic plant from Spain and North Africa yielded violet, lilac, purple and peacock blue. Yellow came from saffron and the roots of Far Eastern plants; browns and other earth tones from Sienese stone.

The painter's most expensive color, and the hardest to use, was ultramarine, made by soaking powdered Far Eastern lapis lazuli stone several times to draw off the color. The first yield, a rich violet blue, was the best and most expensive. Patrons specified the grade of ultramarine they were willing to pay for--at one, two or four florins an ounce.

Finally it was time to turn the ground pigments into paint. "Behold the humble egg," Lippo said, holding one up. "It's cheap, readily available, quick to dry, and easy to store and keep clean. It's also extremely durable on the panel, and won't fade. Now mix the pigments with egg yolks and water."

Lippo and his helpers painted with brushes made from miniver, hog, or other animal fur or bristles. Like every painter, Lippo built a wide collection of brushes in different sizes and shapes.

Because the gesso was absorbent and dried quickly, Lippo slowly worked one limited area after another, carefully controlling his strokes and the amount of pigment on his small brush. He built up the painted surface gradually with layers of underpaint, finally applying the top colors.

As when he had first begun to draw with Lorenzo Monaco, Lippo still felt most pointedly alive when he painted. He celebrated the pulse of his creative spirit when he sat, brush in hand, before an unfinished panel. Religious paintings were no mere decorations, but strong, deeply moving icons, thought to contain some of the power of the holy figures they portrayed. To paint a religious painting was, in effect, to cast a spell. Hadn't some saintly painted images been known to perform miracles? Lippo found it astounding that paint, often made from humble elements of the earth, when applied to simple wood, could result in something so mighty.

Sometimes the knowledge of such possibilities burdened Lippo. He left it to others to say whether his works inspired and transformed those who saw them, and glorified God. He preferred to think of his painting as the contribution that excused him from monastic demands he didn't care to fulfill. Other monks tended the garden, prepared herbal medicines, taught the novices, or copied sacred manuscripts. Lippo painted. Yet he knew that if his father had lived, he surely would have followed him into the butcher shop, and never once picked up a paintbrush.

Months later, when the Carmelite Madonna and Child was complete, Lippo applied delicate highlights of white pigment and a series of tiny finishing brush strokes. Then the work was allowed to dry thoroughly before varnish was applied.

The painting showed what Lippo had learned about naturalness and color from Masaccio. But he had added his own personal, human feeling--the Madonna had the face of a peasant girl, gazing into the distance. The angels, too, had round, earthy faces, like the impish boys of the streets near the monastery. The Carmelites hung the piece above the altar dedicated to St. Angelo in the church transept.

For the Carmelites at the monastery of Selve, between Florence and Empoli, Lippo painted a small panel picture of the Madonna enthroned among angels, and Sts. Michael, Bartholomew and Albert.

Lippo's spirit surged with the praise heaped on these works. People called them lively in tone and color, amazingly detailed, and simply but effectively conceived. The praise Lippo treasured most was that his figures were natural and throbbed with life--qualities Masaccio had valued above all others.

The praise made Lippo's decision easy.

"Frate, I am leaving the monastery," he told the prior.

The Madonna and Child Enthroned with Four Saints.
From left, St. Francis, the Medici patron saints Damian
and Cosmas, and St. Anthony. The Medici commissioned this altarpiece for the Chapel of the Novices in
Santa Croce.

Chapter 4

I absolutely walk on the smooth flags of Florence for the mere pleasure of walking, and live in its atmosphere for the mere pleasure of living... I hardly think there can be a place in the world where life is more delicious for its own simple sake than here.

Nathaniel Hawthorne

They were sitting in the prior's little office, with its writing desk, two plain wooden benches and a crucifix on the wall--the place where they had first met, and had struggled with their differences so many times.

"We both know I was never meant for this life," Lippo continued. "I've got to get outside these walls, as Fra Lorenzo did, so I can do more with my painting. And, well, of course you know the other reasons I must leave."

Frate Jacopo hoped that the enormous relief he felt didn't show. "It saddens me that you found no comfort within these walls," he said. He opened the Bible that always sat on his desk, and turned a few pages. "'Arise, shine; for thy light is come, and the glory of the Lord is risen upon thee.'" He looked up from the book. "Remember that, Fra Filippo. Some will scorn you for leaving this place. But perhaps God sent you to earth to praise Him through your painting. I hope you find contentment out there." They embraced.

Lippo gathered his few possessions from his cell and walked out the monastery's huge oak door. He recalled how it once had closed behind him with such awful finality. Now, not even his cumbersome robes could keep him from running and leaping across the piazza with joy.

The city that Lippo entered was troubled by war and unrest both inside and out. Only a few years earlier Florence had broken off a new threat from its old enemy, Milan, by allying with Venice. As if peace were intolerable, Florence soon began another war, this time to conquer the stubbornly independent city of Lucca.

The war sprang from Florence's longstanding determination to strengthen its control of Tuscany. Through conquest or purchase, Florence dominated Arezzo, Cortona, Montepulciano, Volterra and other towns, and their surrounding farmlands. Pisa was conquered as an indispensable outlet to the sea for Florentine goods. This domination also discouraged rivals, protected the city's earlier gains, and defended trade routes. Florence, the city so obsessed with liberty, did not care to extend that privilege to its neighbors.

At first the war against Lucca was popular with the Florentines--Lucca's rich territories spread from the mountains to the Ligurian coast. But when Milan aligned with Lucca, Florence floundered, and the war became an enormously expensive disaster. Rising opposition to this war made the position of Florence's ruling faction, the Albizzi family, increasingly tenuous.

The gap between rich and poor was growing. Most of the capital and all the political power lay in the hands of the Albizzi and the oligarchy around it: the members of the wool makers' guild; the big landowners; the Uzzano merchant and banking family; and the Strozzi family, the wealthiest bankers in Florence. Together they controlled elections to the ruling councils, and dominated Florence's domestic and foreign policy. About three quarters of the population, both peasants and urban workers, had no political voice, and spent their days struggling against starvation, illness, and violent death.

It was not a profitable time for painters in Florence. The financial crisis caused by endless wars, and the institution of a property tax, both served to limit commissions. Besides, the trade guilds, who provided many commissions, preferred sculpture over painting---sculpture could be placed outdoors, or on the outside of buildings, enabling the competitive guilds to show off their patronage and taste.

Lippo's habits kept him worse off than other painters--what little money he had usually went toward women and drink.

He put together just enough money to rent the ground floor of a tiny house on Borgo San Frediano, named for the Florentine district where it traced a muddy path, not far from the Carmelite monastery.

Lippo could not imagine himself dressed like Florence's rich young men--"I'm a butcher's son; I have no urge to wear colorful silks and fancy caps." And the artisan's long gown so closely resembled the uniform of the Carmelite order that Lippo decided to continue wearing the religious habit he had grown used to: an ankle-length, loose black tunic tied at the waist with a leather belt, under a voluminous white wool hooded cloak. He also kept the title *Fra*--despite his un-monk-like behavior, the title brought him some small respect, and could be quite useful. He made a strange picture, this libertine in monk's garb, raising his cup at the tavern, and knocking fervently at the bordello door.

In the Tavern of the Wren, he could escape the dreariness of his rooms, and with other young craftsmen and workers, tell baudy stories with the typically pithy Florentine humor, laugh at the human condition, and gossip. Sometimes they sang Dante's verses, or made up songs accompanied by pantomime about everyday themes--perhaps someone setting off to fish or hunt, or a girl gathering flowers.

As each tavern night wore on, and Paola the barmaid brought endless jugs of wine, patrons would sing and dance:

> *Let all who join our company*
> *Now sing with joy and dance with glee.*
> *And though the sunrise finds us spent,*
> *We'll hail the gods of merriment!*

No one indulged in merry-making with more vigor than Lippo. But he paid a price for the tavern nights. In the monastery, to dull the misery he'd felt, he had helped himself almost daily to the altar wine, no matter how ingeniously the sacristan hid it. The habit remained, and it disgusted Lippo's friends whenever they had to half-carry him home.

"Maybe I'll just leave you in the gutter next time," his friend Matteo the blacksmith said.

"I don't know why I should worry. One thing keeps me from sinking completely into the arms of Bacchus--the arms of Florence's women!" Lippo cackled. "I must stay just barely sober to fully enjoy a woman's favors. Ah yes, Matteo, I've got it good. I earn enough to feed myself, but without working too much. I have lots of friends--all this, and Florence, too!" At this last assertion, all Lippo's friends around the table nodded, understanding him well, for, though they had seen no other city, each felt certain Florence was the most beautiful in the world.

Lippo loved to look down at it as he strolled the Tuscan hills. His eyes followed the city's most striking feature--the tower-studded, battlemented brick and stone wall, five miles long and six feet thick, that circled the city in a snug embrace. As if that were not enough protection, the monastery of St. Francis stood guard to the northeast on the hill of Fiesole, and the church of San Miniato al Monte to the south.

Florence had about 50,000 inhabitants--fewer than Paris or Venice, and about half as many as it had before the plague struck in the middle of the previous century. But Florence still counted more people than London or Rome. It had gradually expanded 15-fold beyond the orderly, right-angled city plan of the original Roman settlement. Now it was a tangle of narrow streets overhung with balconies and rooftop cornices and punctuated by piazzas and towers. Lippo could walk across the city in 20 minutes, knowing as he did the many twists and turns between buildings. Some streets were paved and had sewers; all lay dark at night except for the occasional votive candle beneath corner shrines.

Each trade had its own particular street, lined with artisan's tenement houses built of brick or stone, and workshops that opened directly onto the street. Sometimes artisans worked on the street itself, on outside workbenches under awnings. The street was a place for a conversation, an argument, a nap, or to dry out printed fabrics, varnished wood, glue, timber and leather in the bright sunlight.

Many houses were built of gray stone, giving their streets an air of solidity. The palazzi of the rich stood behind severe façades and balconies and had as many as 20 rooms in three stories. Children, servants, retainers and guards of these families could be seen talking and playing around the colonnaded ground-floor courtyards.

Lippo often heard the Florentines praise the architect Filippo Brunelleschi, whose work had given such beauty to their native city. In the ruins of ancient Rome, Brunelleschi had discovered secrets of that city's construction, and used them to design the conical dome slowly rising atop Florence's cathedral. His columned porch for the Innocenti Hospital, and his work on the sacristy at San Lorenzo, showed his fascination with pure geometrical proportions, and his rigorously sober style. His principles of linear perspective came to dominate painting and relief sculpture and brought him great fame.

One day, as Lippo worked in his studio, he looked up and saw a monk in Carmelite robes identical to his own, striding purposefully toward him.

"*Buon giorno*. You would be Fra Lippo Lippi," the young monk said. "At last I've found you!"

"And who are you?" Lippo demanded.

"I am Fra Diamante, son of Ser Feo from Terranova Bracciolini. It's near Arezzo. I've just left the Carmelite monastery at Prato."

"Well, how do you know me?"

"I heard about you from a friend of Lorenzo Monaco's who stayed with us briefly. It fascinated me to know that there was another Carmelite nearby who painted." Fra Diamante paused to set down the cloth satchel he was carrying.

"You see, I joined the brothers nearly eight years ago, mostly because my family had given up on ever finding some worthwhile activity they considered me capable of. I suspect you joined the brothers for similar reasons. I found monastic life wretched, so I began to draw and paint to relieve the boredom. When I heard about you, I left the monastery and came here to see if you might teach me. And at the same time I might be of some service to you."

Lippo, surprised but intrigued, invited the man to sit down. Diamante was 23 years old--three years younger than Lippo. He looked around the studio with merry gray eyes.

"For most of the time I spent in the monastery, I felt quite empty," Diamante said as they shared some wine. "I would sit down for an hour of quiet contemplation, and find I couldn't think of a damn thing to contemplate!"

"I'm glad to meet someone who felt the same way about monastic life as I did," Lippo said. He felt suddenly more confident, less like a freak. He studied the refined patrician features of Diamante's face, so different from his own. He accepted Diamante's offer of help in the studio.

"We'll start in tomorrow. First, there's Florence!"
Lippo said, and he closed the studio's wide wooden
shutters. Then he and Diamante set off down Borgo
San Frediano.

"I grew up on a street right over there..." Lippo
pointed toward Via dell'Ardiglione, "...and that, of
course, is the Carmelite monastery, where I met the
Holy Mother Church, to the great dismay of us both!"

They continued down the muddy street of Florence's poorest area. An old beggar approached them.
Lippo and Diamante each placed a coin in his wrinkled
hand.

"The worst off--beggars, criminals, vagabonds--ah
yes, Florence lacks for nothing!" Lippo said. "Even
slaves--mostly Tartars, but some Russians, Circassians,
Moors. Most of them are servants. A difficult life,
certainly. If they sometimes have more security, and eat
better, than some of the 'free,' that's not because they're
treated well--it's because the lives of so many of the free
are even harder," Lippo said.

They walked in silence, crossing the Arno at
Ponte Santa Trinità. Here, more streets were paved,
and the houses substantial and much grander. "This
area is lousy with fancy palazzi, like that of the Davizzi,
with their paneled walls, grand staircases, rugs, silver....
But let's not talk about the rich! If they weren't such
good patrons for my work, I'd have nothing to do with
them. Right this way is one of my favorite spots in
Florence," and they walked to the old market, stepping
around the garbage in the streets.

They strolled among the merchant's stalls, dodged
the running children, took in the smells of bread, leather
and cheese. Everywhere the streets were crowded and
noisy with people and horses and mules.

Lippo approached a palmist where she sat under a canopy, wearing a dress of red and gold brocade. He handed her a coin, and she took Lippo's hand in her two well-ringed ones.

"You have a long hand with a broad palm--that is the sign of the mischievous. Maybe even a knave or a thief! But what's this here? Ah, this line means you are also a man who creates, a lover of beauty! Perhaps a sculptor or--no, no, a painter!" she said triumphantly.

"Amazing!" Diamante said as they continued walking. "That a line on your hand told her you were a painter!"

"Yes, a line on my hand, and probably the traces of paint, too!" Lippo said.

"You don't believe? Then why waste your money?"

"That poor old hag has to eat, like anyone else. It's no different than giving money to a beggar. Besides, it amuses me," Lippo said.

They turned toward Orsanmichele, where Diamante slowly walked around the building, admiring the statues of saints in niches on the outside walls.

"Donatello's St. George! It's even more beautiful than I had imagined!" Diamante said when he came to the statue and the small marble relief below it showing the saint slaying a dragon. "Such mastery of perspective, and the architectural details look so real!"

"Ah yes, Donato, the son of Niccolò di Betto Bardi. He helped Ghiberti with the bronze doors of the Baptistery, but now he works in marble," Lippo said. "Later you'll see his statues in the faade and bell tower of the cathedral. And Donatello is as witty as he is skilled with a hammer and chisel. I admire the unpretentious way he lives, even if I don't care to imitate it."

They walked on. "And here is the best herbalist in town. Next to that is where I buy cheese and eggs-- the shopkeeper always extends credit to struggling painters. See that candle maker's shop? Don't deal with the shopkeeper--deal with his wife. And in that apothecary is where I buy pigments," Lippo narrated.

"An extremely beautiful courtesan lives here," Lippo sighed as they passed an elegant house. "She's cultured, they say, gracious, witty, and plays the flute so it sounds like a songbird. I can't afford her, of course, but I'll show you a suitable bordello. As I said, Florence has everything--the Commune itself runs three such establishments."

They continued to Piazza Signoria, passed the Palazzo along its north side, and entered the cramped, dim streets of the Santa Croce quarter. Eventually they stopped before the debtors' prison known as the Stinche. Lippo's energetic tone turned ominous. "There's another prison even more evil than this, the Bargello, but the worst in all Florence is the Archbishop's prison." Their anxiety grew with their imaginations. "Let's get out of here," Lippo said.

They recrossed the Arno at its narrowest spot, spanned by the Ponte Vecchio, once the link between northern and southern Etruria. A series of butcher shops lined the bridge on both sides, tiny stone dens where skinned rabbits hung, and servants ordered slabs of pork for their masters.

They returned to the San Frediano, and Lippo took Diamante to the first of what would be countless visits to the Tavern of the Wren. After less than one goblet of wine, Lippo found himself expounding about Florence and the Church.

"Besides countless churches, abbeys, and monasteries, Florentines are so proud of their two orphanages, the home for aged women, a hostel for pilgrims with 1,000 beds--almost as proud as they are of the four public baths! But you were quite right to leave, Diamante, men like us weren't born for monasteries."

"Yet you still wear the habit."

"That's a matter of convenience, both physical and social. And I accept commissions from the Church. It's the monastic life I hate--the rules and regulations, and the hypocrisy of so many who call themselves Christians. But I'll never forget that the Church took me in when no one else would, and helped me learn my trade. When Frate Jacopo let me loose to decorate the Carmelite church and monastery, he gave me a gift that I can never repay," Lippo said.

"And why all the women? They say Fra Filippo has been in more beds than a bedbug!"

"The first time I knew a woman, I enjoyed the evil of it, the fact that it was forbidden. My vows had always been a sham, so I didn't feel bad about breaking them. And the bodily pleasure was so great, I didn't try to stop."

"Why didn't you ask to be released from your vows so you could marry?"

"Marriage would have been impossible for me. You see, I've been left behind so many times. My mother died when I was born. My father died two years later. My aunt left me to the Carmelites. I certainly don't need a wife, who, in her turn, would no doubt leave me, too."

Diamante quickly became Lippo's accomplice in waywardness, even if, to Lippo's occasional disappointment, Diamante didn't indulge as heavily as his master.

Like all of Florence, they loved celebration and drama, and the streets and piazzas of Florence formed their free, open-air theater. The church obliged them with about 30 religious holidays a year. And the city's ruling families willingly spent rivers of money on elaborate religious and civic pageants--it helped distract the masses from their powerlessness.

Of the many celebrations from January to March, during the carnival time before the austerity of Lent, Lippo and Diamante especially loved the games of football. Each side had 27 players, all soldiers or city officials, and wearing silks of two colors. Twelve trumpeters, two drummers, two pipers and four men carrying footballs led the players into the piazza. After paying homage to the leading citizens watching the game, each team gave its banners to the referees and the players took up their positions.

Once the ball was kicked off or thrown in, the game careened into a melee of thundering feet and colliding bodies. Observers cheered hysterically whenever a player, using hands or feet, got the ball into the opposite goal. The side that lost had to carry its banner dipped, but no one was surprised if a banner was torn in the rage of revelry.

On March 25, the day the Florentines regarded as the beginning of the year, they celebrated the feast of the Annunciation. Lippo and Diamante joined a boisterous crowd gathered one year in Piazza San Felice, where the architect Brunelleschi had designed a spectacle: a globe-shaped apparatus surrounded by two circles of angels that seemed to float above the piazza. Suddenly the angel Gabriel emerged out of the globe and flew down to the piazza in an almond-shaped machine.

The effect was breathtaking, and the superstitious crowd shook with awe.

All outdoor plays required similar mechanical ingenuity. Actors were suspended on strings, great disks revolved, people went up and down in wooden clouds, sometimes in the glare of large sources of artificial light. A narrator, often in the character of an angel, interpreted the events portrayed. Some actors, such as the Prophets in the Annunciation play, remained on the stage between appearances, sitting in chairs and rising to speak their lines and move around.

Lippo and Diamante preferred the performances of an itinerant storyteller known as Enrico. They stood in a crowd of tanners, dyers, armorers, weavers, smiths of all kinds, and other laborers around Enrico's little platform whenever he came to Florence.

"I call upon the Lord Jesus Christ and the Holy Trinity to direct my words. My esteemed friends, I am honored by your presence, which dignifies the very paving stones on which you stand." His round body vibrated with energy under a gaudy red and green jacket and hose.

He plucked a chord on his lute, and played a quick melody softly as he spoke. "Ages ago, even before Caesar, there was an old king of Mesopotamia who had a beautiful daughter. She had eyes like emeralds, hair shiny and black as when the sun shines on a raven's wing, and as for her face and figure, well, my friends, the angels themselves working day and night could not have designed a more entrancing female.

"Every young man in Mesopotamia desired Luisa, the king's daughter. They argued, they duelled, they jousted," the lute music slowed, "for the privilege of asking the king for Luisa's hand.

"But one man desired her more than the rest, with a desire that was different," a low, steady strumming, "and that man was--" furious strumming, then silence--"the king himself! Yes, beautiful Luisa's father!" Enrico resumed a sad but determined melody, while the weight of his words made the crowd fidget and groan in disgust.

"One night he told her of his desires, and Luisa fled the castle in fear. Her father pursued her relentlessly, past vineyard and farm, over stream and hill, until the girl could stand no more." Agitated strums of the lute.

"Passing a farmer's cottage, she asked if she might borrow an axe. 'For what, fair lady, might you need an axe?' the farmer asked. 'Oh, I cannot tell you, the wickedness of it is so great!' Luisa cried."

Enrico paused, playing dramatic tunes on his lute, until the crowd begged him to go on.

"The farmer handed the girl an axe, and she, before the horrified farmer could stop her--" pause and wild strumming-- "chopped off her left hand!"

Some in the crowd clutched their throats, others let out little howls.

"She ran screaming into the woods, but her father, still in pursuit, caught up with her. He took one look at the ugly stump of her left arm and ran back to his castle, his desire snuffed out forever."

"But what of the girl?" someone called to Enrico, who stood stroking his beard.

"Ah, my friends, would I leave the story unended?" And Enrico began to play a cheerful melody.

"The girl fell into a deep sleep there in the woods, and when she awoke, the kind farmer and his wife were kneeling over her. 'It's a miracle,' they said, 'by the grace of God,' they said, for her left hand had been restored to her arm as perfectly as before. She stayed with the peasants a while, until she heard that her father had not only lost his sinful desires but repented, and she returned in happiness to her father's castle."

Enrico's audience cheered, and gave generously as he passed his hat.

Florence's spring festival began May 1, when young people danced in the piazzas, in couples or threes or large circles. Young women asked young men to dance. The dancing continued all day and all night, and the wealthy made several changes of clothing, hairstyle and jewelry. People also carried flowering branches in procession, to celebrate the rebirth of nature. Fireworks, tournaments and wedding feasts followed, climaxing in Florence's greatest celebration--June 24, the feast of St. John the Baptist, the city's patron saint. On the day before, silk and gold banners decorated shops and the faades of palazzi.

Toward noon, the clergy, bearing sacred relics, led a procession from the octagonal Baptistery named for St. John, through the city and back again. Behind the clergy marched laymen dressed as saints and angels, and the guilds and lay confraternities carrying their banners. In the evening, civic leaders, workers, and peasants, singing in solemn tones, filed into the Baptistery to light candles of offering.

On the day itself, a less reverent procession took place--gorgeously painted chariots, masked allegorical figures, giants on stilts, beggars and nymphs and prophets on horseback, pipers, drummers, trumpeters, bowmen and foot soldiers all marched to the Piazza Signoria. Angels fought devils. God the Father rolled by on top of a wooden tower and peered out from behind a cloud to watch the spectacle.   Wagons carried 100 gilded, revolving models of towers, symbolizing the tribute paid to Florence by its subject-cities. The towers were covered with low-relief figures of horsemen, soldiers, dancing girls, animals, trees, and fruit. Flags of the cities flew from Palazzo Signoria's commanding façade, and representatives from each city presented gifts of candles.   Lippo and Diamante relished the spectacle and celebrated as gleefully as any children.

The feast climaxed in a horse race through the city streets. A high tension hummed among the people lined up along the race route as they waited for the starting signal--three strokes of the bell in the Signoria tower.

Horses often threw and trampled their riders, and sometimes spectators were injured. The winner received the palio, a piece of crimson fabric, trimmed with fur and fringed with gold and silk. It was said to be worth 300 florins.

The long day ended with a bonfire. A visitor once summed up the celebration this way: "The whole city is given over to revelry and feasting, so that this whole earth seems like a paradise." And at the center of public feasting and carousing in Florence, one always found Lippo, guzzling great drafts of life as if each gala were his last.

He and Diamante also found quieter amusements: visits to the botanical garden at Careggi, or to see the lions in the menagerie near Palazzo Signoria. Lippo and Diamante, like all Florentines, held the lions there in special esteem and linked the lions' fates to their own, for the lion was the emblem of Florentine independence. A large litter of lion cubs meant prosperous times ahead, and the sickness or death of a lion was an omen of catastrophe.

Lippo's studio began at the street itself, like most Florentine workshops. He preferred to sit close to the street as he worked, to take advantage of the light, and to greet any passersby he knew. Inside, two long tables and a series of shelves held a confused collection of glue pots, rags, linen and parchment strips, brushes of all sizes, knives, ceramic jars holding pigments, and wooden panels of various sizes and stages of completion. The studio was dimly lit, but the lively talk and activity of the young apprentices kept away gloom.

One morning Diamante sat at a studio workbench facing the street, making brushes from hog's bristles. He worked slowly and methodically, trimming the bristles with scissors, then lining up the brushes according to length as he finished them. When he had a tidy row of 15 brushes, he looked up and saw the merchant Francesco Scolari picking his way through the mud of Borgo San Frediano.

"Lippo, here comes Francesco Scolari! Now don't argue with him! When he asks about the marriage portrait of his daughter that you've been dawdling with, tell him you'll finish it by the end of next week!" Diamante said.

"Next week? Why? Are we late with that project?" Lippo asked.

"Are we late?" Diamante's voice rose in exasperation. "Lippo, Scolari's daughter is about to give birth to her firstborn! Yes, we're late!"

"All right, all right," Lippo said, as Scolari's figure cast a shadow into the studio.

"*Buon giorno*, Messer Scolari!" Lippo said. What are you doing in our humble district today?"

Scolari didn't remove his cap. He narrowed his eyes at Lippo under a lined forehead.

"It positively infuriates me that I had to come at all, Fra Filippo! I have sent numerous servants here to demand that you complete the marriage portrait I ordered last year, but you've ignored them all! You were to finish it 10 months ago! I'm sick of waiting!"

"Messer Scolari, if you wish I'll give you back the advance you paid me, and you can commission some other painter. Why not Federico Valli, or Giuseppe Bembo?" Lippo said, naming two distinctly minor Florentine painters.

"*Santo Cielo...*" Scolari muttered as he took another step closer to Lippo and started to raise his right arm. Diamante jumped up from the workbench and inserted himself between them.

"Messer Scolari, it is indeed regrettable that the portrait was not finished in time for your daughter's wedding. It will be finished by the end of next week. I will personally bring it to your home," Diamante said calmly.

Scolari stepped back. "It had better be finished by the end of next week. Otherwise, we'll let the magistrate handle this," and he left the studio.

"What a silly rube!" Lippo said, and turned back to his work.

"Lippo, the man is right! He shouldn't still be waiting for that portrait!" Diamante fumed.

"Oh, he's just like all the rich. His main goal in life is to decorate both his villas and his servants in the showiest way possible, especially if his nearest neighbors are doing the same. But I can't complain too much. Men like Scolari keep painters in business," Lippo said.

"Yet you treat them terribly! Arguing over pointless details--taking so much longer than necessary to finish things--and that's the second lawsuit threat you've had this month! Sometimes I don't know how you manage to get any commissions."

"It's simple, Diamante. It's my skill. The rich are no longer satisfied with works that are merely decorative--now they want to own something they can show off as a 'genuine Lippi,'" he replied.

"Oh, and of course your modesty helps, too," Diamante said. "It's a good thing you have me around to keep the peace."

"That's why we work together so well," Lippo said, and he did appreciate Diamante's diplomatic way with people--it freed Lippo to concentrate on his painting. He thought it was some sort of miracle, that after having resigned himself to working alone for at least a few years, an agreeable collaborator had dropped into his life as suddenly as a cloudburst.

As much as he loved Florence, Lippo, ever restless, one day suggested that he and Diamante leave the city for a while to explore Padua. He had heard about Giotto's frescoes in the chapel of the Scrovegni family, and wanted to see them. Dante had praised Giotto in the *Commedia*. Although Giotto had died nearly 100 years before, all the painters Lippo knew still learned from his works, and Masaccio had often invoked the name.

But Diamante declined, saying he wanted to go to Terranova instead, to visit his family.

The distance to Padua was more than 100 miles, first through the Tuscan hills, then across the valleys of the Reno, Po and Adige rivers. Bandits were a constant worry, and Lippo was quite lucky not to encounter any. He walked most of the way, occasionally charming a farmer into letting him ride in the back of a wagon. He stayed overnight at monasteries among monks who knew nothing about his past or his tendencies. They saw only his Carmelite habit, and heard the pious tone he'd learned to inject into his voice whenever it suited his needs.

Giotto's frescoes covered the interior of the Scrovegni chapel, a space larger than the Brancacci chapel but still intimate. Standing at the entrance, Lippo first saw Christ Enthroned, above the arch leading to the altar. In three tiers of scenes along the side walls Giotto had painted the life of the Virgin and the life of Christ.

Giotto had worked with minimal planning, and this spontaneity had given the frescoes a certain force and charm. Lippo saw that Giotto had been unafraid to experiment with color, light, and shade. His use of perspective was not rediscovered until Lippo's time. And Giotto was a genius at expressing the core of whatever episode from sacred history he painted: the Expulsion of the Childless Joachim from the Temple showed the humiliation of the event in a homely and natural way. In the Visitation, the dignified and sensitive greeting of Mary and Elizabeth expresses the meaning of the story. His figures had a statuesque human bulk, their limbs revealed under flowing garments. Another painter may have handled detail more precisely, but none could improve on the effect of the whole.

Lippo smiled at Giotto's humor: the fat guest at the Marriage of Cana, the boys climbing into trees in the

Entry into Jerusalem, the barking dog in the Retreat of Joachim to the Sheepfolds. How pleasing were Giotto's soft, warm colors, and how true the gestures of his figures!

After seeing such imposing works, painters more humble than Lippo might have thrown away their brushes and paints and taken up shoemaking. But standing in the chapel, Lippo felt inspired and empowered by Giotto's strength, and vowed to do better.

He visited the domed Basilica del Santo, dedicated to the beloved St. Anthony. Soon word reached the prior of the basilica that a stranger in Carmelite robes was spending hours studying the paintings on the building's walls.

Lippo begged the prior to let him add to those paintings, and, after much negotiation, Lippo was commissioned to paint a fresco depicting the Coronation of the Virgin over an altar. The Paduans, satisfied with the work, then commissioned Lippo to paint frescoes in the chapel of the Lord Chief Justice. He painted several other works in Padua, all the while continuing his intemperate ways.

He returned to Florence after three years. He and Diamante went immediately to the Tavern of the Wren to celebrate their reunion.

Many of Lippo's old friends welcomed him--Matteo, the blacksmith; Luca, the tailor; Alberto, the butcher; and several painters and sculptors. Lippo, so happy to be back in his beloved Florence, drank and sang with more gusto than ever.

His friends asked him to describe his travels. Pleased as ever with a chance to talk about himself, he warmed to the occasion with visible glee.

The San Lorenzo Annunciation. This altarpiece was commissioned for the chapel dedicated to Niccolo Martelli, a citizen who financed the reconstruction of the church.

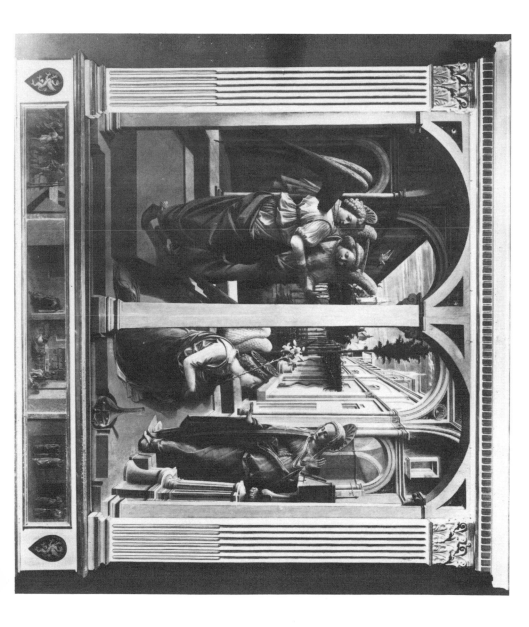

Chapter 5

*Le sue magnificenze conosciute
saranno ancora, sí che i suoi nimici
non ne potran tener le lingue mute.*

*His deeds munificent shall yet be known
So that concerning them his very foes
shall not be able to keep silent tongues.*
                    Dante, *Paradiso*, Canto XVII, 85-87,
                              trans. P.H. Wicksteed

My adventures were so frightening and dangerous that even now I can hardly believe I am
safely home."

The others chuckled, and he continued, his hands flying and jabbing.

"I spent some time in Padua admiring Giotto's frescoes. *O Dio*, they are magnificent! Then I heard that the Basilica del Santo was to be painted. I applied for the commission and naturally was accepted. It seems my fame here had already spread to Padua. Everyone praised my *Coronation of the Virgin* fresco. In fact the

Paduans loved it so much that I received dozens of other commissions. Each one brought me more fame, and more and more people demanded my services. Finally, to avoid death from exhaustion, I started to turn down commissions, to the disappointment of many, and went to the seaside at Chioggia to rest." He paused for a long sip of wine.

"There I met a group of jolly young men who became my close friends. One day the sea was a marvelous and calm blue, and the sun's warmth irresistible, so we set out for a ride in a small boat. The day was so beautiful that none of us noticed a pirate ship approaching until it was too late." Lippo paused to savor the credulous faces of his friends, and they begged him not to prolong the suspense.

"This ship turned out to be one of the Moorish galleys frequently prowling those seas. We were dragged aboard that fearsome ship in chains, and tossed into its dark stinking depths."

"At least the experience didn't cause you to lose your imagination," Luca said, and the others nodded and laughed. Lippo ignored them and continued.

"We were taken in that wretched state to the Barbary, and kept in captivity for a year and a half. My friends, in that uncivilized region, we suffered horribly--infernal heat, disgusting food, the weight of those chains. But that was not the worst of it. We also spent months at a time at sea, rowing the galley of our master, Abdul Maumen."

Lippo's friends exchanged doubtful looks but said nothing. The clamor of the tavern surged around them as Lippo, now fully inspired, went on.

"One day I happened to remove a dead coal from the fire of our master's camp. On a white wall I drew a picture of our master in his fancy Moorish costume. When the Moor saw it, he was struck dumb with awe by my cleverness and skill. He was so impressed that he unchained us, and that night we ate at his lavish table.

"My friends from Chioggia left for home the next day. At my request, Abdul Maumen saw that I was taken to Naples. There I rested and slowly regained my strength. I did some painting for King René of Anjou, then, overcome with homesickness, I returned to Florence. Paola, more wine please!" Lippo sat back, palms on the table, and grinned triumphantly. The table exploded at once.

"That's the wildest story I ever heard!"

"That really is too much!"

"Unbelievable! Tell me, Lippo, didn't the Moor have a beautiful daughter who fell in love with you instantly?"

Lippo protested that every word was true. Only Diamante sat silently, his hand on his cup of wine.

"Well, Diamante, my dearest friend--do you believe my story?" Lippo asked.

Diamante's voice was calm.

"I believe that whatever happened to you in your time away from Florence, you are, for better or worse, the same Lippo we always knew. Whether this tale is true or not is beside the point. It's simply your way of telling us that you believe your painting to be so superior that even an uncouth person like your Abdul whats-his-name would break into rapture at the sight of it. But, no matter! We are all reunited, and I must say this year's grape is exceedingly fine!" He raised his cup.

By 1436, after 14 years of construction, Brunelleschi had finished crowning the cathedral of Florence with his magnificent conical dome, pure and elegant in its lines. The scholar, Leon Battista Alberti, said the dome "rides high in the heavens and can shelter all the people of Tuscany." It made the cathedral dominate more than ever the center of Florence, like a tiger crouched among toadstools. From a flower sculpted in gold and presented by Pope Eugenius IV, the temple took its name: Santa Maria del Fiore. The cathedral proclaimed the sovereignty and fame of the Republic, and on the day of its consecration, all Florence proudly came to watch.

The Pope didn't have to travel to Florence for the ceremony--he'd been living there for two years, having barely escaped from Rome with his life when Romans rioted to challenge his secular authority. Now, from Florence, he was trying to rule a fractious, divided Church.

A band of woodwind players, dressed in gold, led the papal procession from his quarters in Santa Maria Novella to the cathedral. The Pope's silk-slippered feet needn't touch vulgar earth--he walked on a long wooden bridge hung with blue and white draperies and decked with boughs of olive, cypress and myrtle. In his fanciest white pontifical robes and mitre, the Pope led nearly his entire Roman court--seven cardinals in their bright red, 37 bishops and archbishops in purple, deacons and sub-deacons, prelates, and ambassadors from nearly everywhere. The priors of Florence's monasteries, Florentine city officials, representatives of the 16 city districts, and the heads of each guild, with their honor guards, followed the procession through banner-lined streets. The bells of all Florence's churches began to ring as the procession entered the cathedral.

Florentine workshops, including Lippo's, had been occupied for weeks, making ornaments and drapes to deck the cathedral. The five-hour consecration ceremony included every possible flourish: woodwinds and stringed instruments stormed, incense perfumed the air.

One witness said the choir sang "with such mighty harmonies that the songs seemed to the listeners to be coming from the angels themselves." Lippo agreed with the thousands who attended that it was one of the finest ceremonies ever, and rejoiced once again that he had been born a Florentine.

The Archbishop of Florence, Giovanni Vitelleschi, commissioned Lippo to paint a large altarpiece of the Madonna and Child for his palazzo. Lippo's fellow painters said they'd never seen anything like it: the holiest of subjects, yet placed in an intimate domestic setting. Lippo sat the Madonna and Child on a splendid low-backed marble throne. He surrounded the figures with homey objects: a book, a bed, a window showing a stretch of landscape. Behind the two figures, a corridor led to a courtyard. The asymmetrical composition impressed everyone. Lippo had broken from Masaccio's style, with its simple forms and strong modeling, and set out to create his own: figures and shapes carefully outlined, in a less robust manner. This style greatly influenced others, and placed Lippo among the top painters of Florence.

Slowly Lippo's work began to show the influence of Fra Giovanni, a Dominican monk who lived in a hamlet at the foot of the hill leading to Fiesole. Lippo had first heard about him in the monastery, and had seen the delicate frescoes Fra Giovanni had painted for the monk's cells at the monastery of San Marco. He was affectionately known as Fra Angelico (the Angelic Brother). His workshop was as busy as Lippo's with orders for paintings from private citizens and religious groups.

The two painter-monks might have become close friends. But artistically and temperamentally, Fra Giovanni and Lippo sat continents apart, for unlike Lippo, the spirituality apparent in Fra Giovanni's paintings reflected his own devotion.

"Fra Giovanni, Fra Giovanni," Lippo sang mockingly to Diamante after some painters had left his studio at the end of one of their frequent gatherings. "Did you hear it again, just now? I tell you, I am sick and tired of being told how much I've been influenced by Fra Giovanni."

"You both have a good command of figures, brilliant color and design, and you're keen observers of nature. You've been to San Marco--you've spent hours looking at Fra Giovanni's work. Is it surprising that you may have picked up something from him?"

"Oh, sure, Fra Giovanni's work at San Marco. Yeah, I've seen it. So sweet and delicate. And then there's the Madonna he painted for the linen makers' guild, with its doll of a Child, dressed much too fancifully for the son of a carpenter. His Madonnas are beautiful, but they're not human; they're more like angels. Fra Giovanni hasn't tried to understand what Masaccio taught--he consciously ignores it, in fact. And don't forget that Fra Giovanni has taken precious time from his prayers to come here, and to the Carmelite church, to see *my* work. Did it ever occur to anybody that he might have picked up something from *me*?"

"Come on, we'll be late," Diamante replied, setting down his empty wine cup. "The guild always starts its meetings on time."

"I hated joining the Carmelites and I just know I'll hate joining this, too," Lippo said, throwing on his cloak as they headed out the door. "And the guild had better not ever come poking around my studio. It might not be so bad if we had a guild of our own. As it is we painters are held in such low esteem that we have to join someone else's--the guild of the physicians, apothecaries and spice-dealers--for the silly reason that the spice dealers sell us our pigments!"

Both knew they had no choice. The Signoria had decreed that all painters must join the guild, or receive no more commissions. The guild was responsible for holding the painters to professional standards, making sure each painter used durable materials, and seeing to the training of future masters. The guild also set guidelines on the pricing of works--its most contentious duty.

When, to Lippo's delight, the business of the meeting ended, and he was about to invite everyone to join him at the nearest tavern, one painter brought up the issue of wages.

"I think 20 to 40 florins, depending on the size, is an appropriate price for an altarpiece," the painter said.

"Are you crazy, or just doltish? That's much too low!" Lippo protested. "I got only 40 florins from the Guelph party for my altarpiece for Santo Spirito, and then I found out that Fra Giovanni got 190 florins for his altarpiece for the linen makers' guild! I was furious! My altarpiece was much more elaborate than his and had many more figures, and it was larger!"

"But Fra Giovanni's works show his devotion and piety," the first painter observed.

"*Devotion and piety?*" Lippo spluttered with indignation. Are we to set prices based on the purity of a painter's soul, or on the quality of his work?" he demanded.

At once, accusations and retorts flew up and bounced off the stone walls. Insults flickered the lamp's flame. Insinuations and wisecracks rebounded from table to ceiling. "Can we get back to our purpose here?" the head of the guild pleaded in vain.

"I hope I never meet a nastier band of knaves," Lippo said to Diamante later as they walked the darkening streets toward home. "Maybe Florence is too small to have so many painters--it leads to too much conflict and intrigue."

"Among the things I've learned about Florence since I arrived are that Florentines are known for their wit, and Florentine painters are known for their mutually malicious tongues. It seems to be something of a civic tradition," Diamante mused.

As Lippo struggled to get along with the painters' guild, his church, too, strove to make a union of convenience. The two great churches of Christendom, the Roman Catholic and Greek Orthodox, had been mired in quarrelsome disagreement for six centuries, mainly over doctrinal differences. But by the late 1430s the Ottoman Turks, after pecking away at the Eastern Empire for generations, stood nearly at the gates of Constantinople. The Eastern Emperor, John Paleologus, appealed for help, and was even prepared to submit to the Pope's dominance if warriors from the Catholic west would help save the empire from disaster.

Pope Eugenius realized that the chances for reconciliation of the two churches had never been better. But church unity was not the Pope's only aim. A church council was already meeting in Basel, and its delegates wanted to come to terms with the Eastern Church on their own, without the Pope's participation. Worse, at least for the Pope, the Basel council also wanted to reduce the Pope's income through some radical changes in the finances of the Roman Curia.

So to head off both possibilities, the Pope convened an Ecumenical Council in January 1438 in Ferrara, about 70 miles north of Florence, to consider the reconciliation of the churches. The Greek Orthodox Patriarch and hundreds of delegates accompanied the Eastern Emperor to Italy.

Reports soon reached Florence that Ferrara was overcrowded and very cold, and that the delegates were quarreling about procedures and religious rites.

The Medici family, which had succeeded the Albizzi as Florence's most powerful clan, suggested Florence as a larger, more pleasant alternative site for the Council. The Medici knew that it would reflect honor upon Florence if the churches achieved unity there. Besides, closer contact with the rulers of the Eastern Empire would bring new trade to Florence. When the plague broke out in Ferrara, and the Medici promised the Council delegates free accommodations, they immediately accepted the offer.

An eager crowd of Florentines, decked out in their finest clothes, lined the streets of the city to watch the entrance of the Eastern Emperor and the Greek Orthodox Patriarch. Old men, physicians, lawyers, merchants and bankers wore long red or black cloaks that buttoned down to the feet, unbelted, with long wide sleeves and a hood, or a cap with a long strip of cloth to be thrown over the right shoulder, or wrapped around the neck if the weather grew cold. Among Florence's rich young dandies the preferred outfit was a kind of long jacket, belted and hanging down over the hips, made from sumptuous cloth and embroidered. On their legs they wore snug-fitting hose of wool, silk or velvet that reached to the waist, sometimes with legs of differ-ent colors. Their capes could be pink or purple, or patterned brocade, edged in velvet. They wore close-fit-ting boots almost up to the knees, with a border of silk or velvet over the fine leather. They glittered in their gold chains and jewelled daggers, and scented gloves covered the many rings of their fingers.

The varied and extravagant display of Florence's women always fascinated Lippo--and not only because of the warm treasures beneath the fabrics. For this occa-sion the women reached new peaks of splendor in their dresses of silk, velvet or brocade, colorfully embroidered, in every shade and pattern. The typical dress had a close-fitting waist and full gathered skirt, and was often decorated at the hem with cloth of a different color. The belt was trimmed with gold or silver buttons, pearls or precious stones. Over all this the wealthy lady wore a long, elegant sleeveless overdress, in a different pattern and color. A rich woman's shoes were made of the finest leather, silk or velvet, embroidered with pearls, colored glass and silver and gold thread.

Those women who could afford it adorned themselves with jewelry and trimmed their hoods with lace or ermine. Hair considered too dark was dyed blond, or covered with a wig of white or yellow silk. A single long braid was wound round the back of the head, and ringlets fell down over the ears. Skin that was too olive was bleached; too-rosy cheeks were powdered. Everyone wore perfume.

The carnival atmosphere attracted Lippo and Diamante, who stood along the street among other painters and artisans. The excitement intensified when trumpets blared to announce the arrival of the Emperor and the Patriarch, and an entourage of 700 bishops, theologians, scholars, interpreters and officials.

The festive mood dimmed when a light rain began to fall. In minutes a fierce winter storm descended, battering the city with torrential rains. The thousands of observers ran from the streets, clusters of people watching from rooftops were driven down, and flags hung bedraggled where they had flown gaily minutes before. The trumpet fanfares faded to mournful wails carried away by the wind.

But the curious were later rewarded. Frequently over the next six months, two short but entertaining parades wound through Florence to the church of Santa Croce for the Council's deliberations: the Patriarch and his entourage from their quarters in Palazzo Ferrantini on Borgo Pinti, and the Emperor and his court from Palazzo Peruzzi, near Santa Croce. The sight of these bearded men from Constantinople, accompanied by their Moorish and Mongol attendants and strange animals, delighted the Florentines. Many painters, including Lippo, sketched the visitors' opulent clothes and bizarre head-dresses.

During the intervals between Council sessions, Florentine scholars and their Greek counterparts met for long conversations. Among the Florentines one might hear the ironic skepticism of Carlo Marsuppini, respected for his command of Greek, or the gentle piety of the Camaldolite monk Ambrogio Traversari, translator of

Diogenes, or the sharp argumentative tongue of Poggio Bracciolini, the skilled Latinist and critic of church corruption.

As the Medici had predicted, contact with the Greek scholars stimulated the already growing interest in classical texts and philosophy, especially the study of Plato. The Greek Archbishop of Nicaea, Johannes Bessarion, was persuaded to remain in Italy where he was made a cardinal. Gemistos Plethon, a great authority on Plato, also agreed to remain for a time in Florence.

In July 1439, after delicate compromises, the Roman and Greek churches celebrated their decree of union. Cardinal Cesarini for the Catholic Church, and Bessarion for the Greek, solemnly read their agreement in a ceremony in the cathedral. But Lippo had paid no attention to the Council's deliberations and did not attend the ceremony. By the time the Council ended, problems of a quite different nature had engulfed him.

He and Diamante went to the Wren one rainy night after a long day of work. Diamante soon became entangled in an argument with friends over some minor point of Florentine politics. Lippo, bored and tired, returned home alone.

As he was building a fire of pine logs, he heard a knock at the door. It was a girl, about 16 years old, shabbily dressed and veiled against the rain.

"My mother is very sick," she said.

"Child, I'm sorry, but I don't administer last rites anymore, since I left the Carmelite monastery. Go there to find a priest for your mother."

"No. She said it must be you, Fra Filippo," the girl said firmly.

Lippo looked at the girl curiously, wondering why anyone would insist on his ecclesiastical services. But something in the girl's tone, and the pleading in her eyes, made him reach for his cloak. It wouldn't hurt to see the poor child's mother for a moment. Then on his way home he could stop at the monastery and send someone to perform the ritual he no longer had the heart for.

The child led Lippo into the poorest streets of Florence. They walked past blocks of wooden tenements that looked more pitiful in the dark steady rain. Finally they turned down a miserable alley and into a house.

Five younger girls huddled around the fireplace. Lippo walked over to a straw mattress on the floor in the corner. An oil lamp burned beside it.

"Lippo," said the woman lying on the mattress, as she reached out to him with a thin white hand. At once the painter saw something familiar in her gaunt face.

"You don't recognize me. I'm your sister, Piera."

Piera! Lippo's aunt had told him he had an older sister, but he had no memory of her. She'd been adopted when their father died and taken to Pisa, he had heard, and he never troubled himself to find her.

"I didn't want to bother you. But, because of the children, I had to find someone, you see."

"Piera, if you can talk without too much strain, please tell me what has happened to you all these years," Lippo said.

She spoke slowly, pausing occasionally for breath.

"When Papa was dying, Aunt Lapaccia promised him she would raise you, and the Noldini family agreed to adopt me. You don't remember but they were good friends of Papa's. We lived in Pisa. They treated me well, and when I was 17, I married Antonio di Filippo, a shoemaker. We had six daughters. But he died of influenza last year, and I could barely support us."

"Why didn't you come to me then?"

"You have a reputation as one of the best painters in Florence. I would have been ashamed to show up suddenly in your life, a poor relation and all. But now I'm dying, and I have to set pride aside, and be sure that my daughters will be cared for," she said.

Lippo squeezed her hand. "Yes, I'll provide for them," he said. He didn't tell her that he had no idea how he'd keep that promise.

They were silent for a few moments. Lippo did not want to tire his sister further, but there was something he had to ask.

"Piera, you must remember our mother. What was she like?"

Piera managed a tiny smile. "She was beautiful, and gentle, and caring. She wouldn't set mouse traps--- she'd shoo a mouse out of the house rather than hurt it."

The rain had stopped by the time Lippo returned home. He reached at once for a jug of wine and sank gratefully into its refuge from the grief of poverty and loss. "Mamma," he said, as the empty jug rolled from his hand, and he closed his eyes.

For several days Lippo racked his brain, trying to think of ways to keep his promise to Piera. The girls would need not only immediate support, but dowries. He felt helpless.

Six days after he saw Piera, her oldest daughter once again knocked on his door. "Last night my mother died," she said.

"Now, what'll I do?" Lippo said to Diamante when they had returned from Piera's burial, a tiny affair paid for by local charities. "Six girls! Such a burden! They just might have to enter some convent. Plenty of poor girls do."

"Lippo! You yourself were trundled off to 'some convent' and you hated it! How could you wish that on your own nieces?"

"Well, wasn't I Aunt Lapaccia's own nephew? She had no choice..." He paused and gazed out the window. "You're right, I can't do it. But what can I do?" "You could try asking for help."

"More charity? It's embarrassing enough that I couldn't pay for Piera's burial. The thought of more begging is sickening."

"Write to Piero de'Medici--his family often helps painters. It's worth a try."

Writing was hard for Lippo, and this letter was especially difficult, because it required humility, some-thing even the Carmelites had not been able to teach him. He had to swallow two goblets of wine before he could face the task.

> *I am without a doubt one of the poorest frati of Florence. God has left me six nieces to be married, all useless and infirm. I'm all they have. If you would advance to me a little grain and wine to sell, it would give me great joy. I would never ask for myself, but I beg of you with tears in my eyes, for these poor children.*

But Piero refused. For the next few months Lippo struggled to provide for his nieces, giving them money when he could. He came to resent the load more and more, and was less embarrassed each time the girls had to turn to charity for their daily bread.   It never occurred to him to curb his spending on women and drink to help them. When he had a chance to take on a new apprentice, he didn't hesitate.

"I am Francesco di Stefano," said the young man who stood before him seeking an apprenticeship. "Everyone calls me Pesellino, after my grandfather, the painter Giuliano il Pesello, who raised me. I was his assistant until he died last month." An aura of quiet contentment surrounded the youth.

"Yes, I knew your grandfather. I've visited his studio on the Corso degli Adimari. How old are you?" Lippo said.

"Seventeen. I was orphaned at a very early age," Pesellino volunteered.

"So was I!" Lippo said, then instantly regretted having revealed something so personal. He began to talk hurriedly about studio procedures, the work at hand, and other mundane matters. Pesellino accepted the conditions and they agreed that he would begin work in the studio the following day.

Then a silence fell, and Lippo thought Pesellino would turn to go. Instead the young man ran his fingers through his reddish blond hair and said, "Indeed, it's sad never to know one's father or mother."

At once Lippo dropped his guard. He poured out the story of his birth and boyhood--the streets, Monna Lapaccia's house, the dreadful days in the monastery. Pesellino, in turn, told Lippo what little he knew about his parents, taken by the plague, and all about his grandfather, who the young man had loved dearly, and now mourned intensely.

"Perhaps he had little to share about painting, but he was generous with what he knew," Pesellino said. "You never forget your first master."

From then on, the two shared as with no others their worries, their sorrows and hopes. They would talk in the studio late at night while watching the fire die, or on long walks in the Tuscan countryside. Lubricated with wine, they talked about their orphaned lives or the art market, or debated which Florentine painter was the greatest, after Lippo, of course. Diamante was the man to share Lippo's forays into tavern and bordello, but Pesellino was the one Lippo could reveal himself to, knowing he would receive no judgment, no criticism, only unconditional friendship.

"Another apprentice, Lippo?" Diamante said. "And I suppose you're going to pay him a small salary, as you do to all the others?" he asked.

"Yes, the usual small salary, and I wish it could be a large one instead," Lippo replied.

"Lippo, you should be ashamed--taking on this expense while your nieces turn to charity to keep from starving!"

"How I handle my family responsibilities is my business," Lippo snapped. "In fact I have just received an important commission that should help financial matters quite a lot."

The highly regarded cleric Francesco Maringhi had hired Lippo to paint a large altarpiece for the church of the Benedictine monastery of Sant'Ambrogio in Florence. It would be almost as wide as two young boys were tall, and would depict the Coronation of the Virgin.

Lippo set the entire studio in high gear. He even hired extra assistants and two carpenters. He slowed work on less important jobs--some decorated banners and shields, marriage chests, various plates and drapery.

      One day a stranger, a well-dressed, middle-aged man, appeared in Lippo's studio. "I am Pietro di Michele," he said, then turned to look at the unfinished Coronation altarpiece. Lippo felt oddly uncomfortable, and covered the panel with a cloth.
      "What can I do for you?" he said to the man.
      Pietro di Michele adjusted his purple cloak. "I work for Cosimo de'Medici."

The Sant'Ambrogio Coronation. It was commissioned for the high altar of that Florentine church. The original, elaborate wooden frame has been lost.

Chapter 6

*Now, indeed, may every thoughtful spirit thank God
that it has been permitted to him to be born in this
new age, so full of hope and promise, which already
rejoices in a greater array of nobly-gifted souls than
the world has seen in the thousand years that have
preceded it.*

Matteo Palmieri, *Della vita civile*

The man knew he needn't say more. Cosimo di
Giovanni de'Medici was the uncrowned prince of
Florence. Masses of cheering crowds had greeted
him upon his return to Florence from exile in 1434. In
Florence, wealth counted for more than breeding, and
Cosimo's father, a banker, had left him a fortune. The
shrewd Cosimo had increased the fortune through
methodical bookkeeping and imaginative investing in
commerce and industry as well as banking. The house
of Medici had bank branches across Europe; popes and
royalty were among its customers.

Of more interest to Lippo was Cosimo's reputation for patronage--he understood painting and sculp-

ture, and generously supported painters and sculptors he considered worthy.

"And why has Messer de'Medici sent you here?" Lippo asked Pietro.

"He knows your work, and wants you to paint for him. He asks that you come to the Medici palazzo on Tuesday, in the hour before sunset."

Lippo didn't hesitate. "You may tell Messer de'Medici that I'll be most honored to meet him." Pietro nodded and left.

As Medici family patriarch, Cosimo was the dominant, though unofficial, force in Florence's government. He rarely held public office, preferring to rule by pretending not to rule at all. Under Cosimo's wise guidance, Florence's social rivalries were relatively calm, and external relations unusually stable.

Lippo knew that Cosimo loved talking with scholars, theologians and philosophers. When experts on Plato arrived in Florence years before with the Ecumenical Council, Cosimo was so fascinated that he founded an academy for Platonic studies, and spent much time on the subject himself.

Lippo remembered the other things he'd heard about Cosimo: cool businesslike manners, some knowledge of Greek, keen and alert mind, outstanding taste, quick wit. He took pleasure in music, and was a good judge of character.

Though Lippo cared not a whit for power or those who held it, he knew that working for Cosimo de'Medici would mean major commissions, enormous prestige, and money. He relished especially the thought of enough money to comfortably maintain both a studio full of apprentices and his wanton style of living, while also providing for his poor nieces.

So Lippo approached the Medici palazzo on Piazza del Duomo several days later with great hopes. It was a modest home for such a powerful family, crowded with offices and counting houses for the family business.

A servant brought Lippo to Cosimo's study. Between two tall leaded windows stood a long table with carved lions' feet, holding manuscripts, an hour glass, sheets of parchment and seals. The room contained not a hint of luxury or comfort--no painting, no carpet, no bronze or ivory baubles--just an aura of serious scholarly pursuit.

Cosimo sat at a writing desk nearly covered with manuscripts. He lifted his lean form from his chair when Lippo entered and said, "*Buona sera.*" Only the tiniest hint of kindness showed on his wrinkled, olive-colored face as he spoke.

"I've seen a few of your works and heard a great deal about others. I'd like you to do some paintings to decorate various Medici buildings. You'll have a studio here and all the assistants and apprentices you'll need, and the finest materials. Of course, you can also count on substantial wages," Cosimo said.

In his unadorned clothes he looked more like a simple clerk than a shrewd businessman and subtle politician who ruled a city-state. Knowing the inaccuracy of gossip, Lippo was amazed by the resemblance between the real Cosimo and the man Florence talked about constantly.

Cosimo's impatient expression cut short Lippo's musings. "Yes, I'll do it!" the painter said, in a tone a bit too loud and boyishly exuberant for the dignified air of the study.

Cosimo's well-defined lips under his long nose almost but not quite formed a smile. The two men spoke briefly about procedures and wages, and agreed that Lippo would begin the following week. Then Cosimo stood up.

"You will stay for the evening meal, of course?" It was more a command than a question, and Lippo accepted instantly.

If Cosimo de'Medici looked like a simple clerk, he certainly didn't set a clerk's table. This one sat before a large fireplace and was covered with a long white embroidered cloth strewn with fresh flowers and greenery. The family and guests ate from glazed earthenware plates painted with mythological figures by the city's finest craftsmen, and drank from engraved crystal goblets. Servants brought food in colorful earthenware trays and bowls, and water and wine in crystal pitchers. Musicians played softly in a far corner of the room.

The meal began with melon, then progressed to tortellini in broth, followed by berlingozzo, small cakes made of flour, eggs and sugar.

Those were mere preliminaries. Lippo's eyes widened as servants carried in silver and porcelain platters of roast chicken, spiced veal, boiled kid, pike and trout. Then came the vegetables: broad beans, onions, carrots and peas. The wine flowed continuously, and the bread basket was always full. Dessert was rice cooked in almond milk and served with sugar and honey, along with sugared almonds. Everything was strongly flavored.

Lippo ate with obvious enthusiasm, to the amusement of the more sedate dinner guests at the long table. He began to think that the stories he'd heard about Cosimo's simple, unpretentious style of living were false, until he noticed that Cosimo himself ate and drank little. He seemed to leave all that to his wife, Contessina de'Bardi, who ate with great good humor and pleasure, rarely halting her stream of cheerful talk. Her laugh strained the seams of her fine silk gown.

Twilight had fallen when Lippo left the house and staggered toward home, groggy with wine and horribly overstuffed. But despite the hour, a few friends remained at the Tavern of the Wren.

"Wait till I tell you where I've been today...." Lippo began, pulling up a stool.

Under Medici patronage, Lippo soared into a gloriously creative and prolific period. All around him, Florence was in ferment from the stunningly brilliant activity of its painters, sculptors and architects. The economic difficulties that had stifled art in the previous decade had faded. Now Florence's bankers, merchants, and other people of wealth needed architects to design city houses and country villas, and painters and sculptors to decorate them. The rich also sponsored chapels, and hired artists to adorn them with altarpieces and sculpture. No other city on the peninsula enjoyed such economic power and stability. Florentine merchants, operating large international enterprises, had everyday dealings with such faraway places as England and Burgundy, and through this cosmopolitan intermingling achieved a high degree of education and culture. Along with their wealth, Florentines possessed a new confidence, based on their belief that their city was the heir to the glory of ancient Rome. Leonardo Bruni, Chancellor of the Florentine Republic, said Florentines belonged to an urban civilization destined to pre-eminence and "sufficient and worthy to acquire dominion and power over the whole world."

People had been studying classic manuscripts ever since Rome fell, but only in tiny, private circles. Now, study of the classics was an important part of a good education. A Florentine had to turn to these works to know what the city stood for, and all came to admire the wisdom, philosophy and literature of their ancient ancestors. In Bruni's *History of the Florentine People*, he imitated the style of those classical historians--their flowing prose and literary grace.

This time of renewed interest in classical art and letters was one of curiosity and not of revolt; all fields of study were to be vigorously explored, but tradition was not to be abandoned. In this fertile ground Lippo watched Lorenzo Ghiberti work on his second set of bronze doors for the Baptistery. At the same time Brunelleschi was building the church of San Lorenzo, and Donatello was carving statues and medallions for the Medici. Glazed terra cotta reliefs in a tender style by the sculptor Luca della Robbia began to appear around the city. The architect Michelozzo di Bartolomeo was planning a new choir for Santissima Annunziata. And painters such as Andrea del Castagno, Domenico Veneziano, and Paolo Uccello, all spurred by the revolutionary Masaccio, were adorning church and palazzo walls with frescoes and painted panels.

Hundreds of lesser names were no less industrious. In the artisans' quarters of the city, their workshops turned out painted panels large enough to top an altar, or small enough for a traveling merchant to pack; wooden or marble statues to dominate a piazza or sit on a mantelpiece; silver and gold pieces to grace rich bodies, or for the holiest of church rituals.

The attention to the Roman past led artists to take inspiration from the dignity, elegance and clean, spare lines they found in works of Roman antiquity. In architecture, columns, pilasters and smoothly rounded arches imparted a graceful, uncluttered look, quite different from the high windows, carved pillars, and other complicated, fanciful ornamentation of previous centuries. The classical influence reached painting last, because few classical pictures had survived. Painted figures now looked whole instead of flat and without dimension. They began to fill space in a more solid, natural way, no longer floating like angels. They bore faces one might recognize in one's neighbors, on real bodies full of human warmth. In landscapes, familiar animals and plants surrounded the figures. In interiors, perfect architectural lines and details and correct perspective showed people standing among columns, arches and capitals of the same type one would find in actual Florentine buildings.

Lippo's style, too, took on the characteristics of the new spirit. It had matured beyond a simple mix of Masaccio's grandeur and Fra Giovanni's sweetness. It became his own--an ingenious style that added informality and earthiness, even humor, to the basic form of Florentine painting. His portraits were familiar and un-idealized, and arose from careful study of his fellow Florentines.

And where else could this happen but in Florence? Rome had become a mere local market town, rotting and devastated after years of neglect. Pieces of its ancient splendor were being burned for lime. Venice's exotic mingling of West and East made that city's painters receptive to foreign ideas, but they were of lesser ability and remained stuck in the traditions of previous centuries. In Milan, the tastes of their patrons at court limited artists' ingenuity. In Florence, however, broad-mindedness and freedom of expression prevailed to a degree unknown elsewhere in the region, encouraging artists to seek new paths. They proceeded with boldness tempered by prudence--two proud Florentine traits.

Lippo painted an altarpiece for the Chapel of the Novices that Cosimo had sponsored in the church of Santa Croce. It showed the Madonna and Child enthroned among the Medici patrons, Sts. Cosmas and Damian, along with Sts. Francis and Anthony. The four saints sat as if on a stage, like actors in a religious drama, waiting to stand up and recite their lines. Across the top of the altarpiece Lippo painted rows of red spheres, as on the Medici family's coat of arms. The architectural details he placed in the scene made it harmonize well with Michelozzo's design of the chapel.

Pesellino contributed the predella--a row of smaller paintings across the bottom of the main piece. For these works Pesellino painted the nativity of Christ, the martyrdom and a miracle of Sts. Cosmas and Damian, a miracle of St. Anthony, and St. Francis receiving the stigmata.

When the work was done, Lippo and Pesellino took one of their frequent long walks into the Tuscan countryside. The two painters walked east along the Arno, then north, finally stopping to rest on a shady hill above the village of Mensola.

"You exceeded yourself with that predella, Piselli," Lippo said, using the nickname that meant peas. "Such careful detail!"

"I loved doing it. Maybe my strength lies in those little panels," Pesellino said. "And it's a pleasure to work for patrons who really respect painting--the Medici always want the best materials, never cheap substitutes."

"I like to think they also appreciate great skill-- and that's why they hire me!" Lippo said.

"Not that discussion again! It never fails--put two painters together, and they'll start a debate over the quality of materials and the quality of their skills. Which is more important, which do patrons value more, which *should* they value more? Leon Battista Alberti praises showing the brilliance of gold with plain colors. But many patrons won't have plain colors--they want genuine, expensive glitter, not because it looks any better, but just to show off," Pesellino said, then stretched out on his side in the cool grass.

"But that's slowly changing," Lippo said. "It's encouraging that more and more patrons want evidence of skill, instead of lots of showy and costly gold and ultramarine."

"And did you ever notice how often they have death in mind when they commission something? This novices' chapel, for instance--the wealthy sponsor things like that in the hope of winning God's approval, and swifter entry into His kingdom. And some sculptors spend most of their careers doing tombs," Pesellino said.

"Death. Frightful thought, that," Lippo said, sitting upright. "We'll go to God, who will dispense harsh judgment that lasts for eternity.... "

"So you think about it, too. Who would guess that the fearless Fra Lippo Lippi also spends time worrying about death?" Pesellino placed a hand on Lippo's arm.

"Maybe the way I live is why I worry about death. I don't dare think about how God will judge me. You see, I haven't completely escaped the haunting influence of the Carmelites. I probably never will."

"Always remember, Lippo, that our God is a God of mercy."

They sat in silence, watching a hawk glide across the sky. "Enough of this talk," Lippo said, and jumped up. "There's a vineyard near here where they make the best wine in all Tuscany. Let's go!"

Cosimo showed unmistakable pride in Lippo by sending some of his small paintings to Pope Eugenius IV. Lippo was welcome at the Medici dinner table, and joined the family and its friends in their dances, hunting parties and country outings. Still, Lippo's relationship with Cosimo degenerated. Cosimo, in his methodical, businesslike way, always obtained an artist's agreement to finish a commissioned work for a settled price on an agreed date. But Lippo persisted in his undisciplined ways--he worked when he pleased without regard for time, never letting a commission get in the way of indulging his lust.

One day, his patience pushed too far, Cosimo sent his 21-year-old son Giovanni to the studio with orders to remain at Lippo's side until the painter had completed a solid morning's work. Giovanni sat his enormous bulk down and silently watched the painter's every move. The very sight of the young man disgusted Lippo, with his long Medici nose and bad skin. Soon Lippo exploded.

"I can't work like this!" he screamed, and tossed a paint brush across the room. Surely, Lippo hoped, the youth would flee the studio and tell his father that he would not stay in the same room with a lunatic.

But Giovanni remained in his chair, wearing a mild, patient expression, as if he were quite accustomed to wet paint brushes flying past his head.

Lippo glared at Giovanni and sat down, grumbling, at his easel. He soon lost himself in his painting. Several hours later, after much progress, he noticed that Giovanni had left the studio.

The incident drove Lippo to seek other sources of income, to avoid becoming too dependent on the Medici. He asked the bishop of Florence for a rector's or chaplain's position that would provide a stipend but allow him to continue painting.

The bishop, aware of Lippo's licentiousness and unwilling to take responsibility, passed the request to agents of the pope. The pope had found enchanting the small paintings of Lippo's that Cosimo had sent him. He arranged for Lippo to become the rector of the church of San Quirico at Legnaia, a village beyond Florence's western limits.

It was a nearly meaningless sinecure, low on responsibilities and high in compensation, the kind priests coveted, and not the last one Lippo would have in his life. He visited the church rarely. The other priests at San Quirico had managed for months without a rector, and they simply carried on in the same way after Lippo's appointment. Lippo even had his stipend brought to his studio, to avoid the bother of a monthly trip to Legnaia.

The money provided dowries for his nieces at last, and they all married within a year, to Lippo's great relief. If any of them resented their uncle for his stinginess, they never mentioned it to him.

Still, Lippo remained a problem for the head of the Medici clan. Cosimo couldn't begin to fathom how someone possessing such tremendous talent could squander his time on women and liquor. He lost patience, and vowed to attack the problem head-on.

Early one spring evening, after the apprentices had left, Lippo was surprised to find his studio door locked when he tried to leave. Thinking the latch had slipped accidentally, he pounded and yelled for the house guards.

Finally one came and called to Lippo through the locked door.

"Yes, Fra Filippo, what is it?"

"I can't get the door open, you idiot! Fix the lock and let me out!"

"I'm afraid I can't do that, Fra Filippo."

"Why not, you empty-headed imbecile?"

"Orders from Messer Cosimo de'Medici, Fra Filippo. He said this door is to remain locked for two days so that you might better concentrate on your work."

The words sent Lippo into a rage he had not felt since Frate Jacopo had locked him in his monastery cell. He pounded on the door, screamed, stomped with both feet and howled a long string of curses he had learned as a boy on the streets. Then he kicked over an empty easel, snapping off one of its legs.

"So Cosimo thinks he can lock me in like a pig in a sty and that my work will be the better for it!" he stormed. "Cosimo may control all of Florence, but he definitely does *not* control Fra Filippo di Tommaso Lippi!"

He screamed through the door: "See if I do one more brush stroke of work for you or your goddamn family, Cosimo! I'll see you in hell first!"

He began calculating his escape. One window of the studio overlooked a tiny side street, for the moment deserted. It was perfect. With a knife Lippo slashed the sheets on his cot into strips. Then he tied the strips together and used them as a rope to lower himself out the window to the street, and freedom.

The Tabernacle of the Ceppo Nuovo. This panel hung over the well in the courtyard of the Ceppo Nuovo, a charitable foundation in Prato. In the foreground is the founder of the Ceppo, Francesco Datini, and the foundation's four directors.

Chapter 7

Is this your joyous city, whose antiquity is of
ancient days?
Her own feet shall carry her afar off to sojourn.
Isaiah 23:7

The intensity of his anger at Cosimo filled Lippo
with lust to a degree remarkable even for him.
He hurried at once to the bordello and pounded
on the door, ignoring the looks of the curious. When no
one answered, he pounded again.

"*Porca miseria*, hold on, will ya?" a woman's voice
called from inside.

"Oh, it's you, Fra Lippo," said the woman who
ran the establishment when she opened the door and
saw Lippo rubbing his hands. "I wasn't gonna answer
because I thought it was those dreadful little street
hellions playing a joke, they're always around here, ya
know, a real nuisance...."

"Monna Elena, may I come in?" Lippo said
impatiently.

"We're not yet open for the night's business.
Come back in an hour," Monna Elena said.

"But, Monna, please," Lippo begged.

"Well, all right. Good customers deserve special treatment, I reckon," and she let Lippo in. "Wait in the parlor."

Lippo had spent hours in that parlor with Monna Elena's women, joking, listening to their bawdy stories, basking in their flattery. The heavy velvet drapes, cheap furniture and rugs all offended Lippo's aesthetic sensibilities, but never stopped him from returning.

Finally Monna Elena led Lippo to a closed door in a dim hallway, where he thrust some gold coins into her hand. She disappeared, and he opened the door.

The drapes were drawn, blocking what little light might have come in from the street. A small oil lamp burned beside the canopied bed, where a young woman lay lazily on her back, her long brown hair spread across the pillow. Her face, not yet hardened by her profession, was powdered and her eyes heavily lined in black. She forced herself to smile at Lippo.

"Ah, Fra Lippo! Early today, aren't we?" she said as Lippo climbed onto the bed. The woman wore only a plain linen shift, which Lippo immediately slid up to her waist.

He stroked her thighs hungrily, then, hiking up his robe in one deft movement, mounted her. The bell in the Duomo tower began to toll the hour of seven. He was spent in the time it took to say two Ave Marias.

The woman sat up and straightened her shift. She took a brush from the bedside table and ran it through her hair.

"I knew you wouldn't take long, being so eager. Those ones always finish quick." She yawned.

Suddenly Lippo stood up and headed out the door. With the same intensity that he had wanted a woman moments before, now he wanted to drink.

He spent the next three days in a whirlwind of indulgence, from bordello to tavern and back again. He finally woke up one dawn lying in a gutter on a strange street, unsure of who he was and unable to move. He simply blinked at the paving stones, level with his glazed eyes, and the occasional feet walking past him as the city began to awaken.

Soon one particular pair of feet, in well-kept leather shoes, stopped a few inches from Lippo's nose. Even if he had cared to, his head was much too heavy for him to lift, to see who was wearing these fine shoes.

He heard a voice from somewhere above him. "Are you the painter Fra Filippo Lippi?" it asked.

At the sound of the name a tiny light shone through the fog surrounding Lippo's brain. *Yes, that's me*, he thought--the name uttered above the neat leather shoes. But he could not move his thick tongue enough to speak. He merely shifted his head slowly in a drunkard's travesty of a nod.

"We thought we'd find you in such a state. Cosimo de'Medici would like to see you," the voice said. Then the shoes turned and walked briskly down the street.

Cosimo de'Medici--Lippo grimaced and his stomach turned, whether from the bitter memories aroused by that name or from his hangover, he couldn't be sure. He recalled the locked studio door and his escape with the rope of sheets. Lippo still couldn't remember exactly what he'd done next, though given his throbbing head and filthy robe it was not hard to guess.

With enormous effort, Lippo sat up, still in the damp gutter. He groaned and held his head in two hands. A group of urchins, scampering down the street, paused to laugh at the monk in the disheveled habit and scraggly growth of beard. Lippo scattered them with a snarl of profanity.

At last he was able to stand, and found his way somehow to his house in the San Frediano. He waited two days before calling on Cosimo.

Again they met in Cosimo's study, and again Cosimo got straight to the point.

"It was wrong for me to lock you up. I would like you to come back to your studio here and continue working for me," he said.

"I'm honored but surprised, Messer Cosimo. How can you want such an undisciplined rogue to work for you?"

"Lippo, you and I will never see alike when it comes to working habits. I'm a banker, a trader in bills and balance sheets. But you are a painter, possessed of a holy gift. I have come to realize that artists of genius are celestial beings, to be treated with respect and not used as hacks."

"If I do come back, some things will have to change. I will hold the only key to the studio, and I must be allowed to come and go as I please. And you are to send no one to the studio to watch me work."

Cosimo leaned forward, about to tell this arrogant monk to take his brushes and disappear. Surely he had been generous in even allowing Lippo to enter the palazzo again--genius or not. Then an image came to him--of the exquisite tenderness in the Madonna and Child that Lippo had painted for the palazzo. Perhaps, for such unusual beauty, one had to pay an unusual price.

"Agreed," Cosimo said, hoping they would never have to speak like this again.

"I'll return this afternoon," Lippo replied. "But there's one other thing--I seem to remember a broken easel. You'll have to send a carpenter to repair it."

The patrons of San Lorenzo commissioned Lippo to paint an altarpiece depicting the Annunciation. He enriched it with imaginative details: two angels who accompany the announcing angel, intricate buildings, a lovely glass vase to symbolize Mary's virginity. As he painted a beautifully surprised Virgin, full of animation and spiritual charm, he remembered what Piera had said about their mother--"*She was beautiful, and gentle, and caring....*"

Fiesole called to him. A friend of Cosimo's, Alessandro degli Alessandri, commissioned Lippo to paint an altarpiece for a church at Vincigliata on the Fiesolan hillside. And for the church of Santa Maria Primerana at Fiesole, Lippo painted an Annunciation with an angel of supernatural beauty.

One day Cosimo invited Lippo to spend an evening at the Medici villa at Careggi, northwest of the city. Cosimo had no taste for games or other frivolous pastimes, except for a round of chess after dinner. For him, relaxation meant an occasional evening of intellectual discourse with a few learned acquaintances. He drew up the guest list carefully: at least one writer, some philosophers and scholars, a poet or two, and this night, a painter.

The summer evening was pale-sapphire beautiful. A coach pulled by two white horses met Lippo outside Porta San Gallo. The scent of roses greeted him as he approached the villa on cypress-lined paths. He seated himself with the other guests on the veranda, where an occasional gentle breeze carried the fragrance of sweet magnolia.

Some of the more snobbish among Cosimo's guests wondered why he had invited Lippo--after all, painters belonged to a mere trade guild. They knew that Cosimo's friendship and support for Lippo were remarkable, compared to conditions in other circles--in Rome, painters were lumped together with carters and grooms. But out of respect for their host, these thoughts remained unspoken.

Instead the discussion focused on the subjects in vogue among the intellectuals of Florence: poetry, history, grammar, rhetoric, philosophy, the study of Latin and Greek authors, and a longing for the Roman past. Lippo had not been exposed to serious scholarly discourse since his days in the monastery. There he had been expected mainly to memorize, but even that taxed his abilities. Amid such learned company he was quite lost. He turned his painter's eye to Leonardo Bruni, Florentine Chancellor, alert at age 73, and not so much seated on the veranda as displayed in a splendid red robe. Florentines were used to seeing Bruni and other scholars discussing grammar or literature in the Piazza Signoria, or under some loggia, or in a book shop. Many considered Bruni arrogant, and all agreed that his presence was imposing--it was said that an envoy from the king of Spain once fell to his knees at the sight of him.

The sharp-nosed writer and revered scholar of Latin and Greek had come far since his humble birth in Arezzo. Bruni had studied law in Florence, then amassed a fortune working in Rome for the Curia. He had translated Aristotle from Greek into Latin, replacing the old translations with better scholarship and greater elegance. In Florence's ruling councils, he enjoyed such great authority that he was rarely contradicted. The high-minded Bruni sneered at his scholarly friends who kept mistresses, even as he enjoyed life with his rich and much younger wife.

Florence's ruling Signoria had praised Bruni's Latin *History of the Florentine People*, saying it was "composed in an elegant style." This elegance, this eloquence, was highly prized, especially when used to honor the city, and won for Bruni enviable prestige. As Chancellor, he had introduced admirable reforms, consistent with Florence's growing power. Like others of his circle, he believed that a life apart from the political community was as unthinkable as a life without higher reflection.

Cosimo took great pleasure in the way the scholar told a story. "Tell us about the siege," Cosimo asked Bruni.

Bruni had remained relaxed in his veranda chair. But now, suddenly, intellectual excitement overcame him--he leaned forward, eyes wide, his graceful hands dramatizing his words. Lippo listened as Bruni's voice dropped to a passionate depth.

"With pleasure, Messer Cosimo. It's 1402. Florence has barely recovered from an attack of the plague. Gian Galeazzo Visconti, the despotic duke of Milan, has already taken Perugia, Spoleto, Assisi, Bologna and other territories, and has set his sights on Florence. He encircles the city, determined to starve it into surrendering. In this darkest hour, when Florentines despaired and considered their city lost," he paused, "Gian Galeazzo died! His forces disbanded--the

city was freed! Florentines don't consider this a matter
of chance--it is taken to mean that civic virtue had
triumphed. The Chancellor at that time, my esteemed
master Coluccio Salutati, had taught for years before
that fateful event that Florentines were worthy to be the
New Romans. Gian Galeazzo's death seemed to
confirm that. The question of whether or not to study
the classics was settled."

The group exchanged smiles, both from the merit
of Bruni's performance, and the pride they felt for
Florence.

The next to speak, to Lippo's regret, was Leon
Battista Alberti.

Oh no, Lippo thought, *It's Messere who-does-every-
thing*. For Alberti was a writer, philosopher, architect,
painter, and musician; he had worked for popes and
princes, composed poems and theatrical plays, and it was
said he could throw a ball farther than anyone. He had
met Cosimo upon arriving in Florence in 1434 with Pope
Eugenius IV. His treatise on painting greatly influenced
patrons and painters, and gave the art form some
intellectual respectability. Alberti was Lippo's opposite
in many ways: learned and versatile, while Lippo
shunned learning and excelled in nothing but his painting.

"...Donatello's sculpture, with its dramatic and
expressive qualities, uses early Christian and late Roman
art as sources," Alberti began.

Lippo had once attended one of Alberti's lec-
tures, but slipped out about halfway through, out of
boredom. He considered the man tedious and bookish.
Lippo's eyes and mind wandered.

Cosimo noticed Lippo's distress. When Alberti
paused, Cosimo thanked him, in a way he hoped wasn't

too abrupt. Cosimo then told the group how he, frustrated by Lippo's lack of progress on a project, had locked the painter in his studio in the palazzo. This was a shameful error, he told the group. Then he turned to Lippo.

"So, you do not work according to schedules. But I'm curious to know how you *do* work--have you any method at all?"

Lippo's eyes had glazed over during Alberti's speech; but now, fueled by excellent wine, and flattered by the group's attention, his eyes came alive, and he jumped in readily.

"One couldn't call it a method. Quite simply, I love to paint. Usually, as I work, enthusiasm builds on itself, sometimes with a fervor that is almost frightening. At times like that I forget all else but the work at hand," Lippo said.

"And at other times, Fra Lippo?"

"At other times, which are quite rare, you understand, I can't draw or paint any better than a donkey can, and I spend those hours in the tavern or, uh, elsewhere," he said.

A gentle laugh rippled across the veranda. Lippo's amorous habits were no secret to most of the company.

Cosimo took advantage of the lighthearted mood. He asked one of his servants, a flaxen-haired boy, to play his harp and sing. The boy's sweet voice filled the veranda and carried far in the pure air. Lippo felt joy rise with the song.

Later, as the coach carried him home, Lippo considered the various philosophical nuggets he had just heard. Florence as the heir of ancient Rome? Perhaps many Florentines--not just the elite gathered on Cosimo's veranda--could grasp that. Even in the fields of the poorest peasant, the plow often unearthed Roman coins. But Lippo realized that the rest of it, though pretty-sounding and noble, held no meaning or hope for the illiterate poor--and they were most of the people. The peasants remained needy, ignorant, barely staving off hunger in their stone or mud huts. In the city, the many people who worked in the cloth industry went hungry when the shops closed during wars, plagues, or other bad times for business. The poor and powerless were as likely to learn or care about the discoveries and interests of Cosimo's friends as they were to live in castles by the sea.

The Bartolini Tondo, also known as the *Pitti Tondo*. It is among the earliest of Lippo's paintings in which the Madonna is believed to resemble Lucrezia Buti. In the background are scenes from the life of St. Anne.

Chapter 8

On the side of their oppressors there was power; but they had no comforter. Wherefore I praised the dead which are already dead more than the living which are yet alive. Yea, better is he than both they, which hath not yet been, who hath not seen the evil work that is done under the sun.

Ecclesiastes 4:1-3

When Leonardo Bruni died the following year, Florence descended into a week long orgy of mourning.

Bruni's body was wrapped in a Roman-style toga of black silk and crowned with a laurel wreath. The Republic's leading political figures marched in his funeral procession, along with papal and imperial envoys, clerics, scholars and lawyers. The outstanding statesman and Bruni's friend, Gianozzo Manetti, gave the funeral oration, saluting the "luminous star of Latinity." The city spent more than 250 florins on banners, pallbearers' uniforms, candles, and religious offerings, and commissioned Bernardo Rosellino to carve for

Bruni a marble tomb in Santa Croce, Florence's hallowed burial ground.

Lippo, too, watched the funeral procession, aware that Bruni's intellectual curiosity had helped make Florence such a salutary place for painters and sculptors. Often when passing Santa Croce, he stopped to pay his respects at Bruni's elaborate tomb.

Finally, after seven years, Lippo finished the Coronation of the Virgin altarpiece for the church of Sant'Ambrogio. When Pesellino saw the finished work, he was astonished at the boldness of the scene. Lippo had set the celestial event on a large stage full of earthly and realistic characters. Many of them looked outward, as if aware of an audience, or into the distance--anywhere but at the Coronation itself. Near a corner Lippo placed the cleric Francesco Maringhi, who had died shortly after commissioning the piece. As for Lippo's own portrait, Pesellino's eye wandered to the left side of the panel, where the younger of two monks, his chin in his hand, gazed out casually--inattentive, like the others, to the Coronation.

"It certainly bears your imprint," Pesellino told Lippo as they looked over the finished piece. "Rows of garlanded angels, a crowd of saints in charming colors, all rejoicing in materiality and sensuality. Some of the monks of Sant'Ambrogio are sure to be scandalized."

"Probably. But it's not my fault if they can't see the spirituality there--I simply made the atmosphere human and poetic. And the monks asked for all those saints and angels. You know what an effort it was to fit them all in. Compared to this, the Coronation I did for Carlo Marsuppini looks nearly deserted," Lippo said.

Lippo was paid 1,200 lire for the work, including the cost of materials. It was many times what he'd received from the Guelph party for an altarpiece in Santo Spirito almost 10 years before. The Sant'Ambrogio piece had four times as many figures, and the value of "a Lippi" had risen.

The Sant'Ambrogio piece was the most beautiful work Lippo had ever done, and it strengthened his standing as one of Florence's leading artists. It brought him many new commissions. The Florentine Signoria asked him to paint something to place over the door to the chancellery. The Vision of St. Bernard showed the saint raising his head in awe at the Virgin who appears before him, accompanied by three angels. Lippo was especially proud of this project, and as he worked on it, he also had two separate paintings of the Annunciation in progress.

In the midst of this success, Lippo's friendship with Diamante suffered. Lippo now visited the Wren less often, preferring taverns nearer to the newly completed Medici home in Via Larga, where he had a new studio. Sometimes he spent the night on a cot in his studio, instead of returning to his San Frediano house. Diamante realized sadly that Lippo had moved into a world that he himself could never enter.

One late afternoon, burning with jealousy, Diamante barged drunkenly into Lippo's studio. Lippo was overjoyed to see him, but Diamante only grunted.

"So this is the studio of the great Fra Filippo Lippi, master painter," he snarled. Lippo dismissed the apprentices for the day.

"Sit down," Lippo said when the studio was empty, and Diamante sat as if exhausted. Lippo poured himself some wine.

"Well at least have the common courtesy to offer a guest something," Diamante growled, and grabbed the wine jug.

"And how is everyone at the Wren?" Lippo asked evenly. "Paola, Domenico...."

"As if you care! You're much too good for us now, with this fancy studio and your fine friends. You've quite outgrown us all!"

"It's just a room, that's all."

"Please, Fra Filippo, you were never any good at being modest. In my present miserable state, it's the last thing I want to hear," Diamante said.

"And I don't want to hear your whining!" Lippo yelled.

Diamante stumbled over his words. "You've always sneered at the rich, Lippo--now you work for the richest of them all! Cosimo and his type decorate the city to bring glory on themselves, and to feebly atone for the ruthless way they run things, and there you are, brush at the ready!"

"It's all true, what you've said about the rich. They are trying to give back to the city after taking so much from it. And how lucky for us, the painters-- otherwise, we'd nearly be out of work!" Lippo replied.

At that, Diamante passed out, and Lippo moved him to the cot. Lippo spent that night at home, and when he returned to the studio early the next morning, Diamante was gone.

Lippo and Diamante met by chance several times during the next few months, but never spoke more than the briefest civilities. When their friendship later resumed, it was under most painful circumstances.

Giovanni da Rovezzano aspired to be a painter; he wormed his way into painters' gatherings and frequently visited their studios, but was hopelessly untalented. Out of rare and misplaced pity, Lippo hired Giovanni to make some sketches. In the course of several months, Giovanni turned in dozens of useless pieces, then demanded payment.

Lippo's laxness in business matters meant that no written contract existed, and Lippo could not remember the details of their oral one, either. In any case, he thought he had already paid Giovanni.

"You now owe me 10 gold florins," Giovanni said.

"No, I've already paid you," Lippo replied.

"You have not! I've turned in all these sketches, and I've waited long enough. I want the money now."

"*Porca miseria!* You scoundrel! As if these horrid sketches were worth paying for even once, now you want me to pay for them again? Not on your life! Now get out!" Lippo said.

"Not without 10 florins! I knew I shouldn't have agreed to work for you! I never admired your work anyway, Fra Filippo--only that of the painters you drank with. You can't insult me and cheat me and expect that to be the end of it!" Giovanni was already backing toward the studio door. Lippo was relieved when he slammed his way out.

Lippo decided to head off any future encounters with Giovanni. He wrote out a receipt that said he had paid Giovanni the 10 florins two weeks before, and forged the would-be artist's signature. When Giovanni appeared a few days later again demanding payment, Lippo handed him the receipt.

"What's this? That's not my signature! You've really done it now, Lippo! Forgery on top of your lies and frauds!" He stormed out of the studio. Lippo chuckled and poured himself a cup of wine, sure that he had seen the last of Giovanni.

But the convoluted ways and intrigues of the city meant that some disreputable creatures had highly-placed acquaintances. Unfortunately for Lippo, Giovanni da Rovezzano had friends on Florence's episcopal tribunal.

A few days after Lippo handed Giovanni the fake receipt, four of the archbishop's guards barged into the studio with a warrant for Lippo's arrest.

A practical joke, Lippo thought at first. But the guards' faces stayed as hard and unmoving as the stones of the city wall. Lippo froze at the realization.

"Giovanni!" he gasped, but there was no time to mutter denunciations. "Tell Diamante!" he said to his apprentices, who had gathered together in fear at the rude entrance of the guards.

"Diamante?" they asked, aware of the falling out and months of coolness between Lippo and his old friend.

"Yes, Diamante! Tell him!" Lippo said as the guards took him away.

Old women made the sign of the cross whenever they walked past the imposing palazzo housing the court and prison of the episcopal tribunal, where Lippo was taken. The archbishop's vicar-general, Messer Rafaello de'Primaticci, was yawning as Lippo was brought into the courtroom.

The clerk of the court quickly read the charges against Lippo--fraud and deceit, brought by Giovanni da Rovezzano.

The prosecutor told the court that if the charges brought by Giovanni were not enough, Lippo had offended the city-state in other ways.

"He was ordained by the Carmelites, yet embarrassed his order by openly indulging in pleasures of the flesh. Then he left those sacred walls, to better pursue his sinful life. He's supposed to be the rector at San Quirico in Legnaia, but you'd never know it. And his unreliability in matters of business is well established."

The vicar-general asked Lippo if he had a response. The painter, desperately fighting down panic, and pointing his finger toward the floor, cried out, "I'm not the one who should be on trial here, but my accuser, Giovanni da Rovezzano! He's guilty of gross lack of talent. I could show you the drawings he expects me to pay for twice--you'd see they are worthless!"

The clerk of the court reminded the vicar-general that Lippo was entitled to bring witnesses to testify in his defense. But de'Primaticci, signalling with a bored wave of his hand, said, "Take him away." Lippo looked around wildly for one human face that might defend him, but saw only the callous looks of the guards and judges.

They threw him into a chilly cell that stank of urine. The iron door clanged shut, and when its echo died away, a terrifying silence remained, a hellish void far worse than the chill and the smell. Lippo filled it with his screams.

Then, when the energy to scream faded, came the visions: the rack, hot coals, the gloved hands of a hooded torturer, calmly professional...Lippo had heard tales....

Faces appeared to him there in the dark--Aunt Lapaccia, Frate Jacopo, Diamante--they loomed, accusing him, ashamed of him, then melted. *Abandoned again*! Only the darkness and that ghastly silence remained.

Lippo began to wail and sob like a child. Finally, almost against his will, he slipped into sleep, a sleep that gave no rest, as the twisted visions and the accusing faces paraded through his mind.

At dawn, two guards and a prosecutor returned. "Do you confess to fraud and deceit, Fra Filippo Lippi?"

"No," he said, almost inaudibly, his defiance having barely survived the night.

"Take him, then," the prosecutor said to the guards. They half-dragged a terrified Lippo from the cell, through a maze of shadowy corridors and down some narrow stairs, to a small room lit by torches high on the wall.

Now all the apparitions of the night before hardened into repulsive reality. Lippo saw the rack, the whips, a pan full of glowing coals--and was that a black-hooded figure standing patiently in the shadows? The guards dragged Lippo into the room, where the rack calmly waited in the hideous flicker of torchlight.

"Well, you heard it," the prosecutor said to the guards half an hour later. "The poor bastard's confessed. So get him out of here."

They carried the half-conscious and broken Lippo back up the narrow staircase, through the corridors, and back to the stinking cell.

After about an hour, as Lippo's limbs and guts still silently shrieked with the pain of the rack, a clamor echoed up through the corridors of the prison.

"Are you holding the painter, Fra Filippo Lippi, or not?" an angry voice demanded. "Take us to him," another voice ordered. The argument intensified, until finally Lippo could hear an urgent pounding of footsteps toward his cell. Then the metallic tumbling of keys, and his cell door swung opened. He recognized Pietro di Michele and--Diamante!

Pietro was saying something about having paid a fine. The two helped Lippo out the palazzo's huge front door. Diamante turned to the guards at the gate.

"You beasts, you bastards!" he screamed. "Murderers!" The guards ignored him. "They wouldn't let me see you, wouldn't tell me anything!" he said, but Lippo couldn't hear him. Diamante and Pietro took Lippo to the San Frediano house.

The months of enmity between the two painters vanished. Lippo's pallid face and exhaustion horrified his old friend. Diamante did not let himself think of the tortures Lippo might have experienced. For days Lippo only murmured senselessly and moaned in pain as Diamante tended to him. Pesellino visited frequently, and told Lippo about progress he and the other apprentices were making on various works. But still Lippo said nothing intelligible.

When Lippo was stronger, but still nearly mute, Diamante hired a carriage, and they rode to a stone cottage belonging to Diamante's family, in the country-side near Arezzo.

On sunny days Lippo would sit for hours in the quiet air outside, often closing his eyes to better feel the sun. In that warmth his face softened and relaxed, and he began to speak a little. Diamante allowed himself to hope Lippo would recover soon.

But on rainy or overcast days Lippo sat in the cottage, huddled under blankets, brooding, often moaning from the pain of the rack. He ate little--he seemed to need the sunlight even more than food.

Slowly Lippo regained his strength--Diamante saw it first in his friend's eyes, which finally lost their shocked look. His monk's robe no longer drooped like a wet flag on his malnourished body, but took on its old curves as Lippo's appetite returned.

"The new archbishop--Antonino--that uncultured, barbarous Philistine! This is all his doing!" Lippo raged. "Everyone sees his piously simple life, his humility, his care for the poor--some even call him a miracle worker! Yet it was in his prison where I suffered. And how many others before me? How could Cosimo have such a man as a friend?" He described his ordeal to Diamante in detail. "Oh, Lippo," Diamante said with a sob.

"And I confessed," Lippo said. "The shame of that...."

"Don't berate yourself for that!" Diamante said. "If you hadn't, they would've killed you!"

Diamante returned to the cottage late one evening after a trip to Arezzo for provisions. Along with wine, bread, and fruit, Diamante brought back a tall, red-haired woman.

"Lippo, this is Gianna," Diamante said. "Good night." Diamante left the cottage, closing the door carefully behind him.

Gianna walked up to Lippo and stroked his face. "I hear you've had some troubles. Maybe I can help," she said, and smiled as she removed her cloak.

She was smooth, both of skin and manner, and gently coaxed Lippo until his desire, reduced to a dry stream bed by his trauma, grew into a rushing mountain torrent.

When Diamante returned to the cottage at mid-morning the next day, Lippo was bustling around, straightening the few sticks of furniture, hanging blankets outside to air. Diamante was glad to see his friend smiling.

"You know me well, Diamante. Gianna was just the tonic I needed," Lippo said.

"So, are you going to rejoin the human circus now?" Diamante asked.

"Yes, wretched pit that it is," Lippo said wryly.

They talked about collaborating again, and imagined grandiose projects. While they soaked in this atmosphere of renewed hope, a messenger from Florence rode up to the cottage with a letter for Lippo. It was from Cosimo.

> *I am filled with grief over your ordeal. I was at Careggi at the time of your arrest. Wisely, Pietro di Michele acted in my place. I have settled your legal affairs to the court's satisfaction. My son, Piero, has arranged a major commission for you--to fresco the choir of the parish church of Prato. Please give the messenger your response.*

Lippo took the messenger aside and told him what to say to Cosimo. Then he turned to Diamante.

"We're going to Prato!"

Virgin adoring the Child. Lippo painted this for Lucrezia Tornabuoni de'Medici, to decorate a cell in the Camaldolite hermitage in the Casentino area, east of Florence.

Chapter 9

But by and by, the cause of my disease
Gives me a pang that inwardly doth sting,
When that I think what grief it is again
To live and lack the thing should rid my pain.
Francesco Petrarca, *A Complaint by Night of the Lover*
Not Beloved, trans. Henry Howard, Earl of Surrey

It was a fine Tuscan emerald of a day in May 1452 when Lippo and Diamante passed through Florence's Porta al Prato. Their mules carried painting supplies and sketches, a few personal things, and several jugs of wine. Some of Lippo's apprentices would follow later; others would be hired in Prato.

As they rode, Lippo brooded on the fact that the Prato commission had first been offered to Fra Giovanni. The Dominican had turned down the job, having just agreed to paint the private chapel of Pope Nicholas V in the Vatican. It wounded Lippo to know he had been second choice.

He also thought about his friend Pesellino, who had declined to go to Prato with him.

"I'm glad you have such a large and special commission--surely the best you've ever had," Pesellino had said as he helped Lippo prepare to leave Florence. "But large frescoes are not for me. I've known it for a long time--I really prefer the smaller, more intricate pieces. I've been talking to Piero di Lorenzo di Pratese about starting a studio with him. I hope you don't consider that disloyal?"

Lippo shook his head.

"Piero and I decided that I would do miniatures, marriage chests, birthing plates, and occasional large panels. I will never forget all you have taught me, Lippo, but this is a chance I must take," Pesellino said.

"Yes, do it!" Lippo said, embracing his friend. "Paint your little worlds within worlds. I've always said you have a gift for those fine details. I'm proud of you. *Addio*!"

But now as the road wound toward Prato, Lippo realized how much he would miss Pesellino's affection and honesty. Must life be nothing more than a tedious, rutted path full of departures and sorrow?

Soon he and Diamante passed through Prato's six-sided wall and into its stern and somber atmosphere. Like Florence, Prato flourished, mainly through its textiles, and could boast of a number of painters, sculptors and scholars. But until Lippo's arrival, no painter of the first rank had ever worked in Prato.

Politically, the city was completely subject to Florence, and envious of the vast sums spent there for embellishment of churches and other buildings. So the Pratesi were determined that the parish church frescoes would stand as a monument of civic pride, and were willing to pay Lippo a very high fee.

After renting a room at an inn and stabling their mules, Lippo and Diamante paused in front of the parish church, known as the pieve. Horizontal stripes of white limestone and green marble formed a magical play of colors on the unfinished façade. The most impressive feature was the outdoor pulpit to the right of the façade, a masterpiece by Michelozzo and Donatello. They had ringed the pulpit with reliefs of charming scenes of dancers, and shaded it with a circular stone awning.

Lippo and Diamante walked into the church's sober interior, between the green and white marble columns of the central nave.

"Such possibilities!" Diamante said as they stood in the choir, a space of about 60 square yards. "Look how high these walls are. Is this bigger than any space you've ever painted?"

"Yes, by far. And I intend to make it my masterpiece," Lippo said.

From the beginning, however, the project seemed bewitched. Four committees supervised the work, and all their actions were subject to approval by the town council. As long as the money kept coming and Lippo could buy supplies, the work progressed--that is, when it wasn't held up by structural repairs to the choir walls and roof, or by the installation of a new stained glass window, or by other commissions that couldn't wait, or by extremely cold or hot weather, which made the fresco technique unworkable.

And sometimes the pain from the torture he had suffered throbbed so terribly in Lippo's limbs or gut that he could not climb the scaffolding. Faced with all this frustration, it was a significant consolation for Lippo to have Diamante at his side once again--his collaborator and true friend, who had ignored months of animosity to bring him back to life.

They accomplished little during 1452 except to sketch out the scenes for the frescoes--the life of St. John the Baptist, in deference to Florence, and the life of St. Stephen, patron of Prato and its parish church. While the sketches went through the twisted maze of the approval process, Lippo painted a panel for the Ceppo Nuovo, a Pratese charitable foundation. He painted Sts. Stephen and John the Baptist on either side of the Virgin and Child, and below them, the founder of the Ceppo and its four directors. Lippo also made the stone tabernacle that sheltered the panel in its site over the well in the Ceppo's courtyard.

And then, one Sunday in late winter, Lippo was asked to take the place of the priest who usually said Mass for the nuns of the Santa Margherita convent.

While a deacon read the Epistles, Lippo idly surveyed the faces of the Augustinian convent's novices as they sat opposite him in their chapel. One novice's face made him catch his breath--a luminous oval face, purely beautiful and serene, bearing none of the submissiveness Lippo despised in nuns. Her radiance made her stand out from the others like a lily among cattails.

Lippo couldn't be sure, but weren't her lovely azure eyes clouded by a touch of melancholy? Perfect! It was just the look he wanted for the Virgin he was painting on a tondo, or round panel, for the banker Leonardo di Bartolomeo Bartolini. Never before had Lippo been so glad to be in church.

"*Santo Cielo*, she's so beautiful, so entrancing," Lippo said to Diamante as they left the chapel.

"All right, who is it this time?"

"Didn't you see her? That shining face, those blue eyes? A fine Madonna, and a real, breathing woman, too! I must learn her name."

Slowly the Virgin's face on the Bartolini panel emerged from Lippo's memory of the enchanting novice. She wore the same look of melancholy, as if haunted by a vision of the torments awaiting her son. Everyone admired the beauty in that face, and no one but Diamante guessed where Lippo had received the inspiration.

The work seemed to spur him to other glories. Geminiano Inghirami, the head of the parish church, commissioned a large panel painting showing the death of St. Jerome. In their faces and gestures, Lippo vividly depicted the deep affliction and sorrow of the monks surrounding the saint's deathbed.

He painted a large panel for a convent founded by a Florentine widow, Annalena D'Anghiari. Her husband, commander of the Florentine infantry, had been killed by a vengeful politician. "I'll be a boarder at the convent, now that my husband's dead," she had told Lippo sadly. It was the fate of many widows. "I want something beautiful there with me, that I can see every day, so I never forget that there *is* beauty somewhere in this world."

Her words moved Lippo to great sympathy, and inspired him to pour a special grace into the work--some admirers said this Adoration of the Child rivaled the Sant'Ambrogio Coronation in its beauty. In a mystical, fairy tale landscape, Lippo shone golden light on the Holy Family, as Saints Jerome, Hilary and Mary Magdalene watched from the edges. They said it looked like something out of a dream, as Lorenzo Monaco would paint. Others saw the influence of Donatello in the painted figures that looked as though they were sculpted.

Lippo personally delivered the panel to Monna D'Anghiari for her approval, before sending it to the convent.

"I asked for beauty, and you've given it to me," she said, after looking over the panel briefly. She self-consciously ran a hand over her chestnut hair. Then she dismissed her servants from the parlor, to Lippo's surprise.

When they were alone, Annalena reached out and touched Lippo's cheek with soft fingertips, then drew back, embarrassed. "Tomorrow I enter the convent," she whispered, though there was no one to hear but Lippo. "I have missed my husband so much...it is not a sin...."

Lippo put one arm around her waist and kissed her mouth while loosening the laces of her brocade bodice. He moved his hand over her warm breasts. She smelled like carnations. "It is *not* a sin...." Annalena repeated, as they stepped toward a wooden bench covered with a thick ermine blanket.

"No, of course not, sweet Annalena; it is love, and how could love be a sin?" Lippo whispered. They enclosed each other, folding together their hungry flesh. Lippo remained until darkness filled the lonely parlor, then silently slipped out.

With some money he had managed to save, Lippo bought a small house on Prato's Piazza del Mercatale, a vast open space near the Bisenzio River. Here he could enjoy the color and noise of the fairs held on the piazza twice each year. Here too he had more studio space for his craft and more privacy for his passions--at least as often as his health allowed.

"Lippo, is it any coincidence that your new house is directly across the piazza from the convent of Santa Margherita?" Diamante asked as they sat in a tavern after several hours of work.

"What difference could that possibly make to me?" Lippo replied.

"You forget, Lippo--I'm the one who knows that your inspiration for the Bartolini Madonna came from a certain lovely young nun who happens to live in that convent."

"That never crossed my mind," Lippo said, wondering if Diamante somehow knew that every day he looked toward the convent with longing. "Oh, I forgot to show you this," Lippo said, handing Diamante a small piece of paper.

"'Dismissal of Fra Filippo Lippi from the post of rector of San Quirico in Legnaia, for 'misconduct,'" Diamante read. "So, how come it took them 13 years to notice?"

"It's hilarious, Diamante," Lippo said merrily. "Now just what 'misconduct' could they mean? What dalliance with which Tuscan wife or widow?"

"Could it possibly refer to the many services you didn't perform for the parishioners of San Quirico, or the archbishop's case against you?" Diamante suggested.

Lippo's amusement increased when, a few days later, the Abbess of the convent of Santa Margherita, Bartolommea de'Bovacchiesi, approached him and asked him to accept the post of convent chaplain.

"We don't really need a chaplain to say Mass--any priest can be called in to do that. But the new pope, Calixtus III, has decreed that every convent must have a chaplain. You will have no involvement in convent operations, and are not to go near the sisters." She paused.

"It will be an empty appointment, but we must obey. I am well aware of your, ah, tendencies, and how you neglected your duties at San Quirico in Legnaia. But Cosimo de'Medici has been your patron, and that's no small endorsement. And the bishop has already given his approval. Because the chaplain here will be one in name only, you are suitable," she explained to Lippo.

Her frankness stunned the painter, but he realized she had assessed him with absolute precision. He accepted the appointment. His slightly wounded pride recovered when the abbess hired him to paint an altarpiece for the nuns' chapel.

Thoughts of that beautiful novice, now a professed nun, never strayed far from Lippo's mind. He put on his most pious look and affected a gently beseeching tone.

"Abbess Bovacchiesi, you have a sister in your convent, one Lucrezia Buti, whose features I believe make her perfectly suitable as a model for the altarpiece. I have a large request to make. If it offends you, I do apologize. I humbly ask, if Lucrezia Buti could spare time from her duties, that you allow her to pose for me." Lippo's stomach tightened with fear that the old nun would refuse.

The abbess sat back in her chair to think. "Posing for an altarpiece could be a good and holy deed for a sister," she said after a minute, as Lippo tried not to squirm. "But it might make her worldly--it might make her reflect on her beauty and distract her from the spiritual focus of her life. I must think about this, Fra

Filippo. Come back tomorrow and I will give you my answer," the abbess said.

As soon as Lippo left, the abbess called her secretary, Sister Chiara, into her office. Sister Chiara was used to listening quietly while the Abbess thought out loud.

"Fra Filippo wants to use our Sister Lucrezia as a model for the altarpiece he will paint for us," the abbess said. "It's distressing enough to have him as the chaplain here. Letting him use one of our sisters as a model is quite another matter. You are aware, I'm sure, of the sinful ways he has used his body." Sister Chiara nodded and hoped she wasn't blushing.

"But he's already quite old--he has passed his 50th year. And you saw how plain he is. Sister Lucrezia is 23, well past the age when she would have married if she had not joined our community. Despite her beauty, I believe her devotion and commitment to her vows are sound. However it would not be right to tempt either of them. Sister Francesca, the most trustworthy among us, will chaperon each of the painting sessions. Please tell her. Thank you, Sister Chiara."

When Lippo entered the abbess' office the next day, he was the very picture of humility: hands clasped over his breastbone, holding his face in a way that he hoped expressed reverence. The abbess almost laughed when she saw him.

"Yes, Fra Filippo, you may use our Sister Lucrezia as your model," Abbess Bovacchiesi said. "But I warn you--her face must not appear as the Madonna's. That would be a horrible sacrilege. She could model for the St. Margaret figure instead."

The following week, Lucrezia, accompanied by Sister Francesca, came to pose in the studio Lippo had arranged in his house across from the convent.

"*Buon giorno*, Sister Francesca, Sister Lucrezia," Lippo said, ignoring the onrushing desire he felt as Lucrezia's beauty filled the shabby room. He pulled up a chair for Sister Francesca, and handed Lucrezia a robe of pale violet brocade.

"Please put this on," he said, then turned to his workbench and began to prepare some pigments.

Put this on? Lucrezia regarded the robe with confusion. *Does he expect me to take off my....*

Lippo, turning back and seeing her hesitation, held the robe open and placed it over her shoulders. Relieved, Lucrezia slid her arms into the wide sleeves.

"Now, sit right here," he said, pointing to a wide bench. She easily followed his instructions for how she should sit, the exact way she was to hold her head and her arms.

He stirred egg yolk into dried, ground plant roots. "So, your father was a Florentine merchant?" Lippo asked.

"Yes, Francesco Buti, a silk merchant," Lucrezia replied.

"And your mother, is she still living?"

"No." The old look of melancholy returned briefly to her eyes, the look Lippo had seen in the nun's chapel.

"I'm so sorry. May God rest both their souls."

He gradually added water to the root and egg until he had a pale violet shade, similar to the robe Lucrezia wore.

"And your parents, Fra Filippo?" Lucrezia asked.

"I never knew them. I was raised by my aunt, and by the Carmelites." Lippo picked up a long brush and applied the violet paint to the panel in careful strokes.

"While you paint, Fra Filippo, may I speak?"

"Please do, Sister Lucrezia," Lippo said.

"My mother and father believed in the education of girls. I learned to read--not just for the Bible, but the poetry of Dante and Petrarch, and Boccaccio's *novelle*. Our house was full of books, and there were always lively talks, dances, parties...."

Lucrezia glanced at Sister Francesca, afraid she had displeased her, but the older nun ignored Lippo and Lucrezia to concentrate on her rosary.

Lucrezia began to ask Lippo about his work--intelligent questions about commissions, techniques, and his progress on the frescoes. The convent's rules of silence had made Lucrezia forget the pleasure of conversation. Now, the memory stirred, she couldn't hold back. The music of her voice perfectly suited the light of her loveliness, and Lippo painted with uncommon joy and ease.

Lucrezia began to wonder whether the stories she'd heard about Fra Filippo had been exaggerated. He certainly showed no sign of passion or lechery here. He worked methodically, and his treatment of her was considerate yet businesslike, as she had hoped.

What Lucrezia didn't know was that Lippo soon began to dream of her, and even outside the studio, he thought of nothing and no one else. As the days passed, he longed to stop pretending that his admiration for Lucrezia's beauty was merely artistic. He wanted to be with her as a man with a woman, and soon. What exquisite and unbearable pain, that the most beautiful

Scenes from the Life of St. John the Baptist, in the choir of Prato Cathedral. At right, St. John says farewell to his parents. At center right, he prays in the desert, and at left, he begins preaching.

Chapter 10

Quant'è bella giovinezza
Che si fugge tuttavia!
Chi vuol esser lieto, sia!
Di doman non c'è certezza.

How fair is youth,
which is forever fleeing!
Let whoso will be joyous:
Of tomorrow there is no certainty.

Lorenzo de'Medici, *A Carnival Song,*
trans. Ernest Hatch Wilkins

At that moment, the convent bells tolled, awakening Lucrezia's chaperon and calling the nuns to afternoon prayers. The elderly nun stood up, signalling Lucrezia to do the same. They made brief and formal farewells to the painter and walked out.

You fool, Lippo thought. *She'll never be back, and all because of your crude impulsiveness.*

But even as he reeled in despair, he knew he would wait for her that night in the cypress grove. It had seemed like a miracle when the abbess allowed

Lucrezia to pose for him. Perhaps, by another miracle....

Later that day, just at twilight, Lucrezia sat alone in her white cell in the convent. The silence pressed upon her maddeningly. The other nuns had already left for the procession marking Prato's annual Feast of the Holy Belt. She had told them she would follow soon, and none of them had sensed her confusion and indecision.

The Feast recalled a legend about the Apostle Thomas. According to the story, he refused to believe in the Assumption of the Virgin. He believed she had simply died, not ascended bodily into heaven. He ordered that her tomb be opened, and found it full of lilies and roses. Then he raised his eyes toward heaven and saw the Virgin, who loosened the narrow cloth belt on her robe and gave it to him. The sacred belt, or a piece of cloth that passed for it, had been venerated at Prato for centuries.

Tonight it would be taken from the parish church, carried through the town in its gold case at the head of a long procession, then displayed in the splendid outdoor pulpit. All the Pratesi would then spend an entire night in celebration--eating, drinking, singing and dancing. Already Lucrezia could faintly hear distant voices raised in a hymn to the Virgin as the procession began.

Oh, Queen of Heaven, we praise your name,
All souls on earth your holiness proclaim....

But she thought only about Fra Lippo Lippi's words that midday, words she dared to say out loud only because she was alone: "*I must see you.*" With startling force, the words drove home to her a truth she had avoided for years: that she'd never completely embraced the nun's life. Instead it had been her only alternative when, after her father died, her half brother refused to provide her with a marriage dowry.

There had been no point in dwelling on the fact before--she was stuck with a nun's fate, like it or not. And Lucrezia didn't like it. She found stultifyingly boring the daily round of chores, church services, private meditation, and simple meals eaten in silence. She was sick of having to ask forgiveness for violations of endless silly rules. She was 23 years old, and faced a lifetime of this repressive routine.

Lucrezia knew other nuns who had entered Santa Margherita for lack of a dowry, yet they all seemed to blend effortlessly into the contemplative life. She sensed that no other nun shared her feelings of uselessness, though the rules of silence kept her from knowing for certain.

She sat on her bed, holding a prayer book her father had given her when she learned to read. She fingered the embossed and gilded leather cover, carefully turned the handwritten pages to see the lavish decorative lettering. The book was the only thing she had brought with her to the convent.

As she closed the book, the questions she had asked so many times returned. Weren't there people outside the convent's walls who desperately needed the Church's help--help she was eager to give? Other orders of nuns helped the poor, the sick, prisoners, orphans.... But the Augustinians were a cloistered order, so when she brought these troubling thoughts to the abbess, the older woman said simply, "Pray for wisdom."

Sweet mother of our Lord,
Over the universe adored....

Lucrezia stepped over to her little table and considered the reflection of her face in the water of her washing-bowl. She looked at her fair skin and wide-set blue eyes. Her nose was perfectly sculpted, the mouth small but not prim. All her life, until she entered the convent, people had told her she was beautiful. She had dismissed the notion as something said to women frequently, and not always sincerely.

As twilight descended, Lucrezia looked out her small window onto the rooftops of Prato. She could see the outline of the massive law courts building, the bell tower of the parish church, some smaller churches and tenements. She wondered if there were any place under those red slate roofs where she belonged.

A cat pawed along a nearby ledge. "Hey, *gattino*," Lucrezia called. "I see you don't care about the Feast, either."

Did she dare consider Fra Lippo's proposal? Lucrezia knew well his reputation as a satyr, and that he had scarcely slowed down even now, at age 50. It amazed her that he ever found time to paint.

She also knew there would be no taming Lippo. Even if she went to him tonight, she must never count on him for anything. And he would never need her, because Lippo didn't need any particular woman, and Lucrezia found that thought painful.

But even more painful was the thought of this convent life, with its endless chores and self-denial. Surely just a few more years of it, let alone a lifetime, would drive her quite insane. And far worse than the tedium was the prospect of never knowing a man's touch....

Lucrezia yanked off her veil and threw it down on the bed, revealing blond hair cut short. Through the window the sound of hymn-singing from the parade grew louder and closer--the sound of the life that had once been hers. But her life had changed today with Fra Lippo's impetuous words.

She tucked her prayer book into the folds of her habit. She left her cell and walked down the convent halls and stairs that she had scrubbed so many times, then passed through the iron gate to the street. She glanced back once as if expecting--what? The baying of hounds, the clanking of guards determined to drag her back? But the only sound was the ever-louder singing from the procession as it reached fever pitch.

Send down your grace and tender care
And save us all from Satan's snare!

Lucrezia threw back her head and laughed with delight, the first true laugh she'd had in years. She loved the raw sound of it, and the reckless feeling it gave her. "Satan's snare, indeed!" she said gaily. Under the blackening sky, she headed through deserted streets toward a moonlit barley field south of the town, and the cypress grove beyond.

Lippo stood waiting right there among the pines, and he held out his arms when he saw her. A wave of desire surged through Lucrezia as they embraced and kissed, deeply and with great longing.

Finally, with Lippo's arm tight around Lucrezia's waist, they walked farther into the countryside, rich with the wet earth smell of spring, until they reached a tiny mud cottage. Lippo stopped at the door and looked at Lucrezia questioningly, silently offering her one last chance to turn back. But Lucrezia smiled and said, "Shall we go in, Lippo?"

They entered, breathed the scent of fragrant herbs, and kissed fiercely again as nightingales sang in the fields, under the stars.

Lucrezia had known and craved this destiny from the moment she'd ripped off her white nun's veil. No-- long before that. She had longed for this for years, since before she entered the convent. Still, she was surprised by the magnitude of her thirst. She clung to Lippo, and he to her, and they sank onto a worn straw mattress. Lippo's hands slid expertly beneath Lucrezia's habit to rub her breasts and loins, where the pressure grew and threatened to burst. Her hands moved curiously over his muscular chest and back. With glad abandon, she let him press himself inside her in his frenzied rush. She felt a sharp and sparkling awakening within that moved ever deeper as she absorbed the lilt of their desire, the cadence of passion.

In the intensified heat that lingered after, Lucrezia felt like a bird that had flown too high, to where the atmosphere could barely sustain it, yet in that rarefied place had known a pleasure so exquisite that it could never again quite stand to be earthbound.

They were sitting on a low hill overlooking rows of olive trees heavy with buds, after lingering in the cottage all morning. "Now you've lured a nun astray. Even in your naughty, colorful life, surely that tops all your other exploits," Lucrezia said.

"You're right. When the good citizens of Prato recover from the Feast and learn what has happened, they'll say I've sunk about as far as a man can go. Though it took far less persuasion than one might expect," Lippo said with a sly smile.

"I doubt you could have found a nun more ready to leave the convent," Lucrezia said. "That daily routine--ugh! We were supposed to keep silent almost all the time, except of course to pray, confess our sins and beg forgiveness. As if all that weren't enough, I was required to wear a spiked chain on my wrist twice a week, as penance. I'd had quite enough."

"Just why did someone with your beauty ever enter the convent in the first place?" Lippo asked.

"Because of my greedy half-brother. My father was a very intelligent man, but I'll never know why he entrusted my half-brother to manage his estate. After Papa died, Antonio found out that the dowry to enter a convent was much smaller than the one needed to attract a suitable husband for me. Judas got 30 pieces of silver for betraying our Lord, and the Augustinians got 50 gold florins for taking me off my half brother's hands," Lucrezia said bitterly, and her serene expression vanished. Lippo winced, recalling what he had almost done to his six orphaned nieces.

"And my aunt dragged me to the Carmelite monastery because she couldn't handle me. You and I never belonged behind the Church's walls," Lippo said.

They reflected for a moment on this parallel in their lives, looking across the olive trees and the fields in the throes of springtime. Then Lippo filled the sad pause.

"What a shame if your gloriously beautiful body had stayed hidden forever under nun's robes! I must confess, Lucrezia--I first admired you years ago, when I said Mass for the nuns one Sunday shortly after I arrived in Prato. There you were, with that glowing face, and those delicate hands holding your prayer book! I was so inspired that I went to my studio and painted you from memory. The Virgin's face is yours, on a tondo now hanging in the home of Leonardo di Barto-lomeo Bartolini."

"So when the abbess hired you to paint an altar-piece for our chapel, did you choose me to be your model out of desire?" Lucrezia asked.

"No. The artistic considerations came first. But as soon as you began to model for me, I wanted you so much I could hardly concentrate on the altarpiece."

"It's fitting that we ran off on the Feast of the Holy Belt," Lucrezia said. "After all, the Feast comes from one of the few church legends that's based on a love story." Lippo looked puzzled, so Lucrezia explained.

"The Virgin, at the time of her Assumption, gave the cloth belt on her robe to St. Thomas. Before he died, he entrusted it to an old Eastern priest. The priest's daughter fell in love with a Pratese who had come to the Holy Land as a Crusader. The couple eloped to Prato to escape the old priest, who disapproved of their love. They brought the belt as the girl's dowry. Surely you've seen the frescoes in the church's reliquary chapel--they tell the whole story."

"So that's how the relic got to Prato, if you can believe church legend, that is. In fact the day of our escapade was doubly fitting--on the very day Prato celebrated the Holy Belt, you threw off yours," Lippo said.

They spent the next two days at the cottage, in a fog of bliss. By daylight they strolled the Tuscan countryside, through a tapestry of wild flowers celebrating spring--poppies, daisies, primroses, orchids. Backed by a chorus of meadowlarks, they talked about the

Church, painting, the Medici, their lives. At night they plunged back together into that delightful fire of their first union.

On the third morning Lucrezia awoke early, and realized it was time to face the world she had been happily ignoring.

"But I can't bear the thought of going back into the city," she told Lippo. "I wouldn't mind if I never saw that convent again. And I'm sure the gossip is already going around that I've been absent from the convent for two days. All those curious eyes." She shuddered.

"Do you know anyone in Florence?" Lippo asked.

"Florence? Well, yes, I have a widowed cousin there."

"Then, why don't you go there? When the gossip here dies down, you can come back," Lippo said.

"Come back? Come back to what?" Lucrezia asked.

Lippo feared Lucrezia was hinting that he should marry her. It would be right and honorable, but they both were bound to religious vows, at least officially, and besides, *marriage*! It was Lippo's turn to shudder.

"I need you to continue modeling for me. There are several days of work left on the altarpiece," he said uneasily.

"All right," Lucrezia said. If she were disappointed, she didn't show it.

Lippo said he would make arrangements for her trip to Florence, and left the cottage.

As Lucrezia washed in the water Lippo had brought her from a nearby spring, she wondered idly about her future. Her half-brother had ruined her chances of marriage, and now she herself had rejected the nun's life. Surely her cousin Caterina in Florence would know what to do. Despite the feeling that doors had closed behind her forever, Lucrezia felt happier and more hopeful than ever before.

She rejoiced especially in the passion she had gladly shared with Lippo. His thickset body was not beautiful, but his square face was still smooth for a man of 50 years, and his hands were gentle. Lucrezia knew she'd always keep the shining happiness of these days and nights, even if she never saw Lippo again.

"A woman alone isn't safe on these country roads, of course," Lippo said when he returned a short while later. "And it would hardly be right for me to escort you anywhere. But a farm family nearby is going into Florence today, and they've said you can ride with them. You can meet them along that road," he pointed.

Lucrezia put on a hooded cloak Lippo had offered to conceal her nun's habit. They kissed. "*Addio.*"

"*Addio.*"

Lucrezia headed toward the road to Florence, and Lippo set off across the fields and back to his studio. Looking back, he caught sight of Lucrezia just before she disappeared behind a hill. He smiled.

Lippo tried to work, but the memory of Lucrezia's loveliness made it impossible to concentrate. He found Diamante, and they headed immediately to a tavern.

"I haven't seen you so excited since you first met Cosimo," Diamante said. "What could possibly have happened?"

"I have been with the fairest, most splendid woman God ever created," Lippo said, sighing as he recalled Lucrezia's face and body.

Diamante laughed. It was an old story, something he might have predicted. "So that's what you were doing the past few days. She must be as generous with her favors as she is beautiful," Diamante said.

"She's nothing like that!" Lippo snapped. "This woman is different from all the rest--there's something innocent and pure about her! There couldn't be a better St. Margaret for that altarpiece I've been doing."

Diamante went pale. "Do you mean--that little nun--that's the girl you've been with the past two days?"

Lippo nodded.

"Do you know what this could mean? The penalty for seducing a nun! It could be death!" Diamante fought to keep his enraged voice beyond the hearing of the others in the tavern.

"Well, I'm not worried," Lippo said calmly.

"Oh no, of course, you're not. You're not capable of it. Let's get over to the church--some difficulties came up with the frescoes while you were away," Diamante said.

That evening, having arrived safely in Florence, Lucrezia sat in the home of her widowed cousin Caterina.

"Once the chance to leave that convent life appeared, I had to take it. You wouldn't believe the tedium, the uselessness I felt behind those walls!" Lucrezia said.

"But to run off with a monk! And that rogue Fra Filippo Lippi, of all monks!" Caterina said.

"Yes, Fra Filippo," Lucrezia said wryly. "He's certainly one of God's sorrier creatures, and if it weren't for his painting and his friendship with Cosimo de'Medici, he probably would have been hanged for something by now. But he treated me with a--a tenderness that was quite, uh, quite...."

"Your sainted parents would be despondent!" her cousin said. "Remember how your father always doted on you--hiring tutors, having you taught how to read, while his friends told him so much education was unnecessary for a girl?"

"Yes, he developed my mind, and I'm sure he would want me to use it!" Lucrezia put her hands to her temples, then dropped them in her lap. "What about you, Cati? Will you throw me out?"

"No. I don't approve of what you did, but we'll say no more about it. You can stay here as long as you like," Caterina said.

While Lucrezia and Caterina were vowing never again to mention her encounter with Lippo, Prato could talk about nothing else. Suspicions were aroused as soon as it became known that a nun was missing from Santa Margherita. Then someone overheard Lippo's tavern conversation with Diamante after the tryst. For weeks the event was the top subject of gossip in every home, tavern and shop. Rumors inevitably sprang up.

"They say he grabbed her right out of the convent while everyone was at the Feast!"

"I heard she threw herself at him while posing in his studio, and, Lippo being Lippo, only one thing could happen!"

"It's to be expected from a girl so beautiful. She was probably quite vain!"

"What do you suppose will happen to the old lecher?"

That last question occupied not only the gossips but the magistrate of Prato. The abbess, after seeing Lucrezia's veil tossed on her bed, had gone to the magistrate and demanded Lippo's arrest, certain that Lucrezia had been brutally abducted and raped. The abbess flatly rejected the magistrate's suggestion that perhaps Lucrezia's flight had been voluntary.

Lucrezia had once mentioned the name of her beloved Florentine cousin to the abbess, and after many weeks of prodding the abbess persuaded the magistrate to look for Lucrezia there. He sent deputies to Caterina's house with a warrant for Lucrezia to sign.

"If Fra Filippo Lippi is convicted, he could be executed," a deputy explained.

Lucrezia was firm. "No, I don't want him arrested. I don't want any action taken against him at all. Now if you'll excuse me," and she went behind the house to vomit for the second time that morning. By the time she returned, the deputies had left.

"Well, you're certainly being charitable," Caterina told her.

"Cati, how can I possibly have my baby's father thrown in jail?" Lucrezia asked.

Scenes from the Life of St. Stephen. The parish church at Prato, now the cathedral, is dedicated to St. Stephen. At left, Stephen meets the bishop. At center, he expels a demon from a possessed man. At right, the Pharisees ridicule and disdain him during the disputation in the synagogue.

Chapter 11

Ogni cosa è fugace e poco dura,
tanto Fortuna al mondo è mal constante;
solo sta ferma e sempre dura Morte.

Everything is fleeting, and little endures,
and worldly fortune is inconstant;
the only firm and everlasting thing is Death.
> Lorenzo de'Medici, author's translation

As for Lippo, his only regret about the time with Lucrezia was that it cost him the chaplain's post at Santa Margherita. A small price, he reckoned, for a few nights with the incomparable Lucrezia. Often he closed his eyes to remember her blond hair, her sighs, her breasts like two full moons.

Meanwhile, Lucrezia and her cousin were making plans. "I really don't need Lippo's help. I'll beg on the streets before I'll depend on him," Lucrezia said.

"I know you want to be independent. But the man has fathered your child. He has a responsibility, and you must make him face it," Caterina insisted.

"What do you suggest I do?"

"You must go to Prato while you're still able to travel, before your condition gets any more advanced. When you see him, and tell him what's happened, surely he'll show some decency. I don't think even Lippo would throw you out in your circumstances. And he can't ignore a baby born in his own house," Caterina said.

"He did tell me about a house he owns, away from his studio, in the Gorellina. Why don't we move in on him there?" Lucrezia chuckled. "I can't wait to see his face!"

So the two women borrowed some mules and, with a couple of male cousins as escorts, set off for Prato. Diamante answered when they knocked on the door of the Gorellina house.

"You must be Fra Diamante," Lucrezia said. "Lippo told me about you. I am Lucrezia Buti, and this is my cousin, Caterina Anelli."

Diamante had instantly recognized Lucrezia, from Lippo's works that she had inspired. He stood on the doorstep with his mouth hanging open stupidly, shocked to see her.

"May we come in?" Lucrezia asked, and Diamante stepped aside. Finally he found his voice.

"Please sit down," he said. "Lippo is at the church. I'll tell him you're waiting here for him." Then he raced to find Lippo.

The painter was high on the choir scaffolding when Diamante, breathless, yelled for him to come down. "Not now," Lippo protested. "I'm right in the middle of...."

"Yes, now!" Diamante urged. Lippo gave quick instructions to the assistant standing beside him, and climbed down, grumbling.

"She's here!" Diamante said. "That nun of yours. She's waiting for you at the Gorellina house, right now, with her cousin!" Lippo was stunned for a moment, then he smiled broadly at the memory of Lucrezia.

"I'd better go to her at once. My friend, I'll leave the rest of today's work in your hands," he said to the agitated Diamante.

Lippo was glad that the house was only a few steps from the church. The moment he saw Lucrezia he yearned to press her body against his, but he stood away when he saw the other woman.

"Lippo, this is my cousin, Caterina Anelli," Lucrezia said. "She was just going to the market."

As soon as the door closed behind Caterina, Lippo took Lucrezia in his arms and kissed her warmly. She relaxed against his chest.

"I never expected to see you again," he said.

"And I didn't expect to see you," Lucrezia said. "But something has happened to bring us together. I'm going to have our baby."

"But--from just those few days?"

Lucrezia laughed. "Sometimes that's all it takes! It was something of a surprise to me, too. I thought I didn't come sick on time because of the excitement of leaving the convent. But when I realized we had created life, I was full of joy." She tried not to laugh again at Lippo's confused, almost horrified expression. "I suspect this is all rather foreign to you."

Dizziness overcame Lippo as Lucrezia spoke, and he had to sit down. Fatherhood! The idea was indeed rather foreign. She might as well have told him that he had been named the sultan of Persia.

"When?" he managed to ask.

"It will come in late January."

They agreed that Lucrezia and her cousin would live in the Gorellina house at least until the baby was weaned. To Lucrezia's surprise, Lippo insisted on helping support the baby.

"You don't have to. I can manage," Lucrezia said.

"I *want* to. Sometimes shirking responsibility doesn't give me the thrill it used to. Maybe that's because I'm an old man now. Please let me help you," Lippo said.

As they talked, he began to relax. Lippo told Lucrezia that Diamante would finish the nuns' chapel altarpiece. He talked about the choir frescoes in great detail, describing the figures he had just completed and the technical problems he had yet to overcome. He became so absorbed in talking about his work that he seemed to leave the little room and draw into a world completely within himself.

Lucrezia realized that nothing would ever be as important to Lippo as his painting. The Church had been unable to hold him, and no woman or child would, either. Even though he spoke now of supporting the child, she remained determined never to count on him completely. After all, this man had a well-deserved reputation for unreliability. If she let herself be fooled, the suffering could be enormous.

They lived as a curious sort of family--Lippo, Lucrezia and Caterina. Upon Lucrezia's arrival, Diamante moved into the Carmelite monastery of Prato, but he visited the Gorellina house frequently, often at supper time. They ate the simple foods of artisans and workers--wheat bread, beans, boiled millet, chestnuts, soup, macaroni, wine. If Lippo received a large payment for a painting, they ate their bread with a slice of bacon, or put pork or fowl into the pot.

Lippo's more gossipy neighbors soon discovered the arrangement, but on the rare occasions when their disapproval reached his ears, he brushed it aside. Lucrezia heard nothing on the streets--a woman in her condition did not go out.

From Florence, Giovanni de'Medici, Cosimo's younger son, asked the Pratesi authorities to free Lippo from his obligations on the church frescoes long enough to paint an important commission. Giovanni wanted a three-panelled altarpiece as a gift for Alphonse of Aragon, King of Naples.

Was it just a coincidence that the commission came at this time, or were the Medici, ever Lippo's protectors, trying to ease an embarrassing situation by giving him an excuse to leave Prato for a while? Lippo never knew. That autumn and winter he traveled back and forth between the two cities every few weeks, working in Florence on the Medici commission, and in Prato on various works commissioned by the magistrate's office.

During Prato evenings at home, Caterina often entertained Lippo and Lucrezia with her lute. She was a skilled musician, and blessed with a pure, high voice.

When last I saw my love, and felt his hand
Upon my breast, and knew his blazing kiss,
On high did saints and angels strong command
We soon would part, but soon return to bliss.

One evening in late December, after Caterina had played her lute for them and gone to bed, Lippo and Lucrezia lingered in the parlor, in the light of a single oil lamp.

"Ah, Criza," Lippo said, using the affectionate nickname he spoke only when they were alone. "Your condition has made you more radiantly beautiful than ever! May I...?" He reached one hand toward her swollen womb.

"Of course," she said, and as he placed his hand on her, the baby kicked. Lippo giggled like a child.

Lippo was delighted to have Lucrezia back in his life, but he worried about the peril of childbirth that she would face. If something happened to her.... Although Lippo attacked his work with renewed vigor, disturbed imaginings flitted in and out between his thoughts of pigment and perspective.

One morning in early February of 1457, Lucrezia grabbed her swollen belly and began to howl. Lippo stood over her helplessly.

"Go get Monna Grazia from downstairs," Caterina ordered, then set about comforting Lucrezia.

Lippo returned with the neighbor, grabbed his cloak and fled. He felt faint when he arrived at his Piazza del Mercatale studio. Conflicting emotions raged through him: pride, anger, love, suffocation, and above all, fear.

He could not work. He drank a glass of wine, cleaned some brushes, did some lazy sketches, burned them. He wrapped his white cloak around him against the damp cold and stepped out onto the piazza. It was full of the people of Prato, moving with their customary purposefulness, but Lippo felt distinctly alien, as if he'd stepped onto a stage and didn't know his lines.

He walked slowly toward the Gorellina house and began to climb the stairs, but turned and raced back down to the street when he heard Lucrezia scream. He broke out in a sweat despite the cold.

He thrust his hands deep into the folds of his cloak. He rejoiced when his fingers found a few forgotten coins, and went to the market square to buy a jug of wine. An urge to talk, to make human contact, overcame him.

Lippo poured out to the wine merchant an incoherent story about needing the wine because his wife, who was not really his wife, was having a baby, and he wasn't sure about it, and he had no more wine at home, and....

"Sounds like you've already had too much, Fra Filippo," the wine merchant said. Lippo carried the small jug home as if it were a delicate jewel.

Several hours later he had nearly consumed the wine, and it had broken the jagged edge off the agony of waiting. He fell into a deep slumber.

He awoke late the next morning and approached the Gorellina house, this time hearing tired moans as he climbed the stairs.

"When will this be over?" he asked Caterina.

"No one can say. I'll send word. Now, I've really got to go. Lucrezia needs me."

And she doesn't need you, Lippo thought, incorrectly finishing Caterina's words.

He went to a tavern, where he felt grateful for the noisy banter, the sound of games and laughter. He ate greedily--roast pork, beans, bread, oranges, dates and wine. He returned to the studio in better spirits, mixed some paints and made good progress on a couple of panels.

Just before sunset, the neighbor woman arrived to tell him that Lucrezia had given birth to a robust boy.

Lippo, relieved that Lucrezia had survived the ordeal, slept easily. The next morning, Diamante came to the studio to congratulate him.

"You're certainly not the happiest new father I've ever seen," Diamante said.

"Diamante, I am 51 years old--an old man. I am proud to have a son, but what do I care about babies? I have my work--that's all that really matters to me. And I'll certainly need to work, more than ever, if I have a baby to feed," Lippo growled.

"I can tell you're nervous from the way you're pointing down with your left finger--as if you're accusing the floor of something. But a son should be your greatest joy, Lippo! Just go see the little one."

"When I'm good and ready." He washed, ate, and did nearly two hours of work before setting down his brush. He realized that he was sitting in the very room where it had all begun--where his passion for Lucrezia had grown to uncontainable heights, and where he had asked her to run away with him. He never dreamed his desire would come to this--a helpless woman, and a ravenous little mouth to feed. It was even worse than the burden of six impoverished nieces. He wondered whether this child was the reckoning, finally coming due, for a lifetime of wild carnal liberties.

He began to worry about what Lucrezia would say when they met. He had dawdled so long since he heard the news. What if she wouldn't see him? At first he had cursed the burden of her--now he feared he'd lose her.

With some effort, he pushed back his doubts, and went home. Caterina smiled when she saw him, and nodded toward a draped-off corner of the room. Lucrezia was in bed, holding the sleeping infant.

"I--I'm sorry I waited so long to come," he said, groping to explain. "But you see, I--well, it was just--"

"Come over here and get a good look at your son, Lippo," Lucrezia said gently. "I call him Filippino."

Lippo's fears melted. "He's beautiful, like his mother," he said with a bit of awe.

"With a pudgy face like that? I hope not," Lucrezia said.

In early June a heat wave, thick and sticky as syrup, threatened to crack new plaster, and Lippo had to suspend the fresco work. He went to Florence to work on the Naples altarpiece. Almost as soon as he arrived, he learned that Pesellino was dying of consumption, at age 35.

Lippo went to his friend's side each day, never staying more than a few minutes, or he would be stricken, too. The illness lingered cruelly, through weeks made more painful for Pesellino by the tyrannical heat. He burned with fever, he sweated, and one side of his emaciated chest collapsed. His breath smelled like stale bread. The apothecary recommended sugar, a luxury, flavored with violets, but it did no good.

"Remember that winter when it snowed, Piselli, and we made snow lions in Piazza Signoria?"

"Yes, and some children attacked your lion--and I had to stop you from attacking them!" Pesellino laughed, then a fit of coughing seized him.

"Maybe we shouldn't talk," Lippo offered.

"Us? Not talk? Then I might as well be dead already," Pesellino said.

"You're not going to die!"

"You don't have to pretend, Lippo. I know what's happening to me." Lippo turned away, not wanting his friend to see the bitter anger in his face, and how Pesellino's courage put him to shame. When he turned back, he forced cheer into his voice.

"Good night, Piselli. I'll be back."

"I'll be here. For a while, anyway."

Lippo's anger and frustration returned when he stepped out onto the street. He went to the bordello, but for once he found no pleasure in flesh, and none of the numbness he so desperately sought.

One evening at sunset, as Lippo prepared to leave his friend, the young painter said, "Goodbye, Lippo."

"Don't say goodbye to me! Not yet!"

"Yes, it's time. I've suffered enough."

Lippo went straight to the tavern and got thoroughly drunk. When he was able to stir the next day, he went to Pesellino's house, but it was already hung with black mourning cloth.

He felt his gut start to shake. The muscles in his arms and legs tensed with fury. A fruit vendor had just set up his cart, at the corner nearest to Pesellino's house, and was carefully arranging his lemons, melons and figs. Lippo ran up to him.

"Can't you see someone has just died here? Get off this street at once!" Lippo screamed at the fruit man. "Are you mad?" the fruit seller howled back, his nose inches from Lippo's. "This is my corner! I've got to make a living, you know!"

Lippo stepped back, placed two hands under the edge of the cart, and flipped it over. He watched with pleasure as fruit rolled everywhere and the fruit seller chased it, cursing.

An hour later, sitting under a tree in one of the rare grassy spaces just within the city walls, Lippo saw a boy he knew, the son of a fellow painter. "Giorgio!"

The boy approached cautiously. Lippo smiled and waved him over.

"Want to earn a few *soldi*, Giorgio?"

"Yes, Fra Filippo!"

"Do you know the house of the painter Pesellino? Yes? Good! Take this money to the fruit vendor at the corner near there. Tell him Fra Filippo di Tommaso Lippi apologizes."

During the modest funeral, Lippo's anger turned to an inner hollowness, now that he would never again see the placid face of Pesellino, or hear his voice.

As the priest droned, and incense sailed by, Lippo began to brood about birth and death. In the space of a few months, a son had been born to him and Pesellino had died--two events he could not have imagined just a year ago. Lippo had lived a life of full-speed dissipation, heedless and self-indulgent, yet he lived on, well into old age. Pesellino, 16 years younger than Lippo, had lived modestly and with prudence--and he was already dead. *Poor Piselli!*

Lippo could not draw a crumb of truth from all that had happened. In the monastery he had silently ridiculed the monks who spent hours contemplating such things. How he longed for a bit of their wisdom now! He smelled a bitter whiff of helplessness and doubt. How little humans understood of their own lives, their unfathomable yet unavoidable fates! He pictured humanity as a mass of blind oxen, stumbling around in ignorance and fear, struggling just to survive in the hostile and brutal pit that was Earth.

After the burial Lippo wandered the streets of Florence. He thought about Pesellino's most successful work--a Madonna and Child panel from his last years. The colors glowed like enamel, the shaping of the figures reflected a sure hand, but most important was the emotional force, especially the meditative, melancholic look in the Virgin's eyes. Pesellino had learned from his master to add a human, lyrical touch to Masaccio's monumentality. The work was so popular that copies had appeared all over the city, a thought that gave Lippo odd comfort.

Lippo ended his wanderings at the studio Pesellino had shared with Piero di Lorenzo di Pratese. The studio was closed, in respect for Pesellino, but Lippo found Piero, who showed him an altarpiece of the Trinity and Four Saints that Pesellino had left unfinished.

Lippo was stunned by the beauty and skill already evident in the piece. He told the patrons, the Confraternity of the Most Holy Trinity in nearby Pistoia, that he would be honored to finish it. They agreed, and Lippo arranged for the altarpiece to be transported to Prato.

He was miserable and tired when he rode through the city gate of Prato the next day. At least he had Lucrezia and Filippino to comfort him, and to hint at vigor and hope. Lippo loved especially to watch Lucrezia feed the baby.

The painter was always overcome with the beauty of the scene--Lucrezia's young face, full of love for her child; the blue veins visible on her gorgeous white breast, swollen by motherhood; the baby's concentration as he sucked away. It was a Madonna and Child painting come to glorious, joyous life.

For several months after Filippino's birth Lippo had not approached Lucrezia with his desires--he thought she would need a long rest after her ordeal. Then his grief after Pesellino's death had temporarily stilled his lust. But soon after his return to Prato he began to yearn for Lucrezia's warmth.

Caterina had moved back to Florence when Filippino was six months old. Once the child fell asleep, Lippo and Lucrezia were alone.

"Criza..." Lippo began, touching her hand.

She recognized that tone of longing--the same tone she had heard in the studio, the day Lippo had asked her to run away.

He held both her hands, then pulled her close and wrapped his arms around her. He removed the pins and clips that bound her wavy blond hair, letting fall a soft gentle veil that had replaced the linen one she had thrown off. Lucrezia felt that initial thrill of desire once again as they kissed in the flickering candlelight.

Finally they released each other, just long enough for Lippo to snuff out the flame. "Tallow candles are expensive, you know."

He loosened Lucrezia's dress and let it fall to the floor. He slipped out of the monk's robe he still insisted on wearing. On the feather bed, they explored each other's bodies eagerly, sighed and gasped at the touches as they brought each other to pleasure, then sank deeply into the relaxed sweetness of the aftermath.

But Lippo continued to seek out other women, and Lucrezia was disappointed but not surprised. She reminded herself that she had always known it would be this way. Besides, she knew a few handsome young Pratese men, who climbed her stairs as Filippino slept, whenever a tiny candle Lucrezia placed in one window signalled that Lippo would not be home....

She carried Filippino into the market square when she did her chores. Those Pratesi who recognized Lucrezia and might have sneered their contempt at her instead smiled with approval when they saw the cherubic Filippino. She loved the child more than she loved Lippo, and indulged and spoiled him terribly. He grew into a sweet-tempered boy, and when Lucrezia played with him, her moments of guilt about leaving the convent became rarer.

Without warning, her joy turned to agony one day late in 1458, when Filippino was nearly two years old. He stopped smiling or even focusing his eyes, and his body raged with fever.

She spent every waking minute by his crib, praying. Lippo often sat with her, equally despairing, but he had his work for distraction.

"You've been sitting in that very spot for days now. You must get out of this house," Lippo said to her one evening just before sunset.

"How can I leave him?" Lucrezia asked.

"I'll stay right here the whole time you're gone. There's nothing you can do," Lippo said.

She didn't want to leave, but she felt like arguing with Lippo even less, so she put on her hooded cloak and left the house. Unthinkingly she walked to the piazza of the parish church and circled slowly around it, then stopped at the church steps. Some unknown compulsion drove her inside.

Flickering votive candles in front of the main altar and a few of the side altars dimly illuminated the interior. Lucrezia knelt down at an altar dedicated to the Virgin, laid her head on the railing, and wept.

It's all my fault, she thought as she cried. I left the convent, rejected the good and the holy, and committed sins of the flesh. The happiness I felt with my son was the devil's way of tempting me to continue in unholy pleasure with Lippo and the others. I cannot let my son bear the punishment meant for me. Dear Virgin Mary, I know there is only one way to save my son....

"Yes, Yes, I'll go back!" she wailed aloud. "Please, just let my son live!"

She remained at the altar a while, praying, then dried her eyes and walked home, where she resumed her post beside Filippino's crib.

The next morning, Filippino seemed alert, and she sent for a physician, who said that the fever had broken and that Filippino would probably live.

Lucrezia cried silent tears as she patted Filippino's cheek. Lippo thought they were tears of joy and relief. While Lucrezia felt unbounded gladness for her son, the tears were really for herself--for, while her son would live, she knew her own life was over.

When Filippino was completely recovered, Lucrezia told Lippo, "I'll be leaving soon...."

Herod's Banquet. At left, the head of John the Baptist is placed on a platter. At center, Salomé dances. At right, Salomé presents the head of the Baptist to her mother, while the banquet guests look on in horror.

Chapter 12

Him then I think fondly to kiss, to hold him
Frankly then to my bosom; I that all day
Have looked for him suffering, repining, yea
many long days.
Louise Labé, *Poor Loving Soul* trans. Robert Bridges

L ippo was inconsolable, but he believed that the
promise Lucrezia had made had saved the boy's
life, and must be honored.

Lucrezia left Filippino with a trusted woman
friend. Then, after miserable farewells to him and
Lippo, she went to see Abbess Bovacchiesi and asked to
be re-admitted to the convent.

"I always believed that Fra Filippo held an evil
spell over you," the abbess told her. "I prayed that
someday you would break that hold. There is rejoicing
in heaven over a stray lamb who returns."

"Praise God," Lucrezia said. She didn't tell the
abbess about the promise she had made. The abbess
mistook Lucrezia's mood of melancholic resignation for
regret and contrition.

Lucrezia was required to repeat a year in the novitiate. She was more than 10 years older than most of the other novices and felt awkwardly distinct from them, not so much by age as by experience. Outwardly, Lucrezia was a model novice: quiet, frequently lost in apparent prayer, diligent in her chores, and never shirking small penances. And she never cried, even when her lemon fall of hair was chopped to just below her ears. She kept her sanity through secret acts of defiance. At night, she closed her eyes and remembered the pure pleasure of lying naked beside Lippo, his hungry kiss, his expert hands caressing her and bringing her to exhilaration.

She responded dutifully as the abbess prepared her to renew her vows, comforted by thoughts of her son. It surprised her that she could so easily fool the abbess into thinking that the penitence and remorse she showed were real.

Convents housed many people like Lucrezia and Lippo, who entered religious orders through misfortune rather than choice. Their rebellious act was not terribly unusual. Still, Abbess Bovacchiesi considered Lucrezia's return a personal victory and a testament to her skills as an abbess, as well as a triumph for the Church and the forces of good. So she made sure that Lucrezia's second profession ceremony, in December 1459, was more elaborate than the first.

This time the vicar of Prato and the bishop of Pistoia attended. Candle in hand, Lucrezia knelt before the altar in the nun's chapel, below the altarpiece that had brought her to Lippo, and led to the son for whose life she now took these vows. She sighed inwardly as a white nun's veil was once again placed on her head: *Just like a shroud*, she thought. She was required to read aloud a special list of promises written by the abbess: "Steadfastness, change of conduct, chastity, and obedience to the rules and regulations of the convent." Her face reflected neither the joy the abbess expected, nor the sorrow Lucrezia felt, but remained blank. In the Church's eyes she was now wholly purified and welcome behind its timeless walls.

Lippo, too, was despondent, and looked for solace in the bottle, the brothel and his work. He stayed away from the Piazza del Mercatale house, unable to look across at the convent that now imprisoned his Lucrezia. Fortunately, he had more to do than ever before. He watched over the installation of the new stained glass window in the choir, made to his design, and learned to work in the reduced and strangely tinted light that shone through it.

For a church in Pistoia, he painted an altarpiece showing St. John the Baptist and six other saints. No one seemed to mind that the face of St. Lawrence bore a noticeable resemblance to Pesellino's.

Geminiano Inghirami, head of the church of Prato for nine years, died in 1460. Lippo received a commission to paint four lunettes that would hang over Inghirami's tomb in the cloister of the church of San Francesco of Prato.

He found himself traveling frequently between Prato and Florence. Cosimo continued to commission decorations for the new Medici palazzo on Via Larga. It was a cube of a building, formed from rough rectangular stones and overhung by a wide cornice. The plain façade reflected Cosimo's dislike of ostentation. Around its central courtyard was enough living space for a household of 50 people. It provided abundant work for Lippo and many others.

Benozzo Gozzoli, once an assistant of Fra Giovanni, had been hired to paint frescoes in the palazzo's chapel. Gozzoli called his work *The Journey of the Magi to Bethlehem*, but it represented the arrival of the Eastern leaders in Florence years before for the Ecumenical Council. In the work Gozzoli depicted Cosimo, his son Piero and his young grandson Lorenzo, as well as other Medici family members and associates, coming out to welcome the Eastern Emperor and various celebrities.

But the Medici reserved for Lippo the most important task in the chapel decoration: the altarpiece depicting the Nativity. It was a moody piece tinged by fantasy--a beautiful Madonna adoring her Child in a dark and shadowy forest. Lippo painted the figures in strikingly bright colors that would stand out in the candlelight of the windowless chapel. The infant, lying naked in flowers and grass, bore an exceedingly sweet expression. The Virgin looked down at the Child tenderly, and held the tips of her fingers together in prayer with great delicacy. This sweetness and tenderness characterized Lippo's work more and more.

Not long after, a youth of 15 years, Alessandro di Mariano Filipepi, entered Lippo's Florentine workshop. He was the youngest of a tanner's seven children. His father had earlier apprenticed him to a goldsmith called Botticelli, whose name Sandro adopted. But while working in the goldsmith's shop Botticelli also learned about painting, and after that, gold held no more glitter for him.

The green-eyed Botticelli had a long, sensitive face and sensuous lips, but he was without vanity. Lippo

Rogue Angel

A NOVEL OF FRA LIPPO LIPPI
BY
CAROL DAMIOLI
(1994)

- LIPPO MADE A RELUCTANT CARMELITE AT AGE 8 IN 1414
- SEX AT 15 BECAME ADICTIVE AND HE FOUND MANY WILLING PARTNERS.
- MASACCIO WORKS AT THE MONASTERY AND TAUGHT HIM HOW TO PAINT FRESCOES IN BRANCACCI CHAPEL.
  - HE DIED OF PLAGUE IN ROME AT 27.
  - LIPPO WAS 24 IN 1430
- WORKED FOR RICH/POWERFUL COSIMO DE' MEDICI
- AFFAIR WITH SISTER LUCREZIA BUTI IN PRATO CONVENT
  SHE = 23   HE = 50's
  - SHE GETS PREGNANT! GOES TO LIVE WITH

  COUSIN, CATERINA ANELLI, IN FLORENCE
  - SON = FILIPPINO
  - BABY GETS SICK AT 2 IN 1458. LUCREZIA BARGAINS WITH GOD, BABY LIVES AND LUCREZIA REJOINS THE CONVENT
- BOTTICELLI AT 15 COMES TO WORK WITH LIPPO
  - ULTIMATELY HE WORKS FOR PIERO DE' MEDICI
- COSIMO DE' MEDICI USE HIS INFLUENCE TO HAVE POPE RELEASE LIPPO + LUCREZIA FROM THEIR VOWS, MARRIES THEM + LEGITIMIZES THE BABY. THEY LIVE TOGETHER AS A FAMILY
  - SHE WORKS WITH POOR + SICK AT THE CEPPO
  - 2ND BABY WHEN SHE IS 32 AND HE 59 = ALESSANDRA IN 1465
- LUSTED AFTER 20 YR OLD BIANCA LANDRINI DE'CELANI IN SPOLETO. HE DIES THERE. BODY LOST!

A LOVELY BOOK. GOOD READ ABOUT THE "BAD MONK"

APRIL 2012

saw his younger self in Botticelli's enthusiasm. Under Lippo's influence Botticelli's work became more linear, and softened with a lush palette of pastel shades. It was not long before Lippo recognized the stamp of genius the young man possessed. His skill lay not merely in an ability to imitate his master, but in a rare, original gift. "It's like poetry made visible," a visitor to the studio said about Botticelli's work, and indeed he drew his inspiration from classical literature and Boccaccio. Others praised his superb skills as a colorist, and the harmonious balance of lines and forms in his work.

Not all of this pleased Lippo.

"The boy's a growing blessed genius," Lippo said glumly to Diamante as they sat in a Prato tavern one day.

"And of course, you're jealous," Diamante said.

"If you're so damn smart, how come *you* work for *me* and not the other way around?" Lippo said.

Diamante ignored the bait. "Can't you see what's happening? A certain pattern, a cycle, is being played out here. The great Masaccio taught you--now it's your turn to share what you know. There will always be Botticellis coming along--very few will be so gifted, of course, but if you live long enough, many young painters will challenge you. And while I hate to say it, because your vanity needs no help, don't forget that if Botticelli paints so well, maybe that's a tribute to you, his master."

"Yeah. You may be right," Lippo said, mulling it over.

Over time Lippo came to praise Botticelli freely, without the slightest envy, and he was proud when Piero de'Medici invited Botticelli to live and work in the Medici palazzo.

It was through Botticelli that Cosimo heard the truth about Lippo's adventure with Lucrezia and its aftermath. He hadn't taken seriously the many rumors he'd heard about the affair. But Lippo had confided in Botticelli, who in turn told Cosimo the story.

Cosimo was not one to condemn Lippo's behavior. He knew others did, however, and he thought the couple deserved a chance to make their relationship lawful in the eyes of the Church. Cosimo, more than anyone in Florence, had the power to give them that chance.

In 1461, while Lippo was in Florence working on various projects, Cosimo summoned him to the Medici palazzo. A servant brought him to Cosimo's bedroom instead of his study. Lippo had not seen Cosimo in years, and was a bit shocked by Cosimo's even more wrinkled face and the slowness of his movements. He had heard that Cosimo suffered so much from arthritis and gout that he often had to be carried around the house, and that he spent long hours at his villa in Careggi just sitting in silence.

But today the banker exuded more warmth than he was generally thought to possess. "Lippo, sit down, have some wine," Cosimo said as Lippo entered. "I have something splendid to tell you. I wanted to see you here," he waved an arm into the large bedroom, "because this news is special and personal, and the study is too businesslike for it."

The two men sat at a corner table below mullioned windows. As Cosimo poured white wine into exquisite crystal goblets, Lippo took in the great curtained bed, with its inlaid wood headboard and embroidered red silk bedspread trimmed in gold. At the foot of the bed lay a massive silver-plated wooden chest. A crucifix hung on the wall near the bed, and on a shelf opposite sat the carved wooden head of a woman--perhaps the Virgin.

Other shelves and niches in the paneled walls held helmets, painted terracotta sculptures, and various bronze figurines.

Cosimo said, "I've heard about your elopement and the birth of your son. I know you rightly ignore obnoxious gossips, but for the sake of the young lady involved, I have tried to ease any distress the situation has given her." He took a sip of wine. "I appealed to the Pope, Enea Piccolomini, on your behalf. He's a client of my family's bank. He released you and Lucrezia Buti from your vows so that you could marry." There was a brief, awkward silence.

"You what?" Lippo finally said. Cosimo confused Lippo's incredulity with denseness.

"With this papal brief," he said patiently, pointing to a parchment before him on the table, "His Holiness not only released both of you from your monastic vows, but declared you and Lucrezia to be married. Maybe Piccolomini's old habit of woman-chasing made him especially sympathetic to your case. And oh, by the way--your son is legitimized." Cosimo gave Lippo one of his rare smiles.

"Married," Lippo repeated, trying the word on like a glove, and deciding it was much too tight. Somehow he forced himself to say, "Cosimo, how can I thank you for this? And I'm sure Lucrezia will be grateful, too, and very happy."

But he felt not at all sure as he rode to Prato the next day. He felt joy beyond measure that Lucrezia now was free to leave the convent and return to his side. But marriage! He knew he could not live as a faithful married man--he knew few men, married or not, who were true to one woman, and it would be pointless for him to try. Surely Lucrezia knew that, too. And what about Lucrezia's vow to the Virgin to re-enter the convent in return for her son's life? It was one thing for the Pope to release her from her vows, but would she release herself?

Night had fallen by the time he arrived in Prato. Lippo went straight to the convent of Santa Margherita. Sister Chiara, who finally answered his knock, gasped when she realized who it was.

"Fra Filippo! You are forbidden to enter here!" she said.

"Sister, please fetch the abbess at once," Lippo said. Weariness after his ride from Florence, and his eagerness to get Lucrezia back, had drained what little patience he had.

"Abbess Bovacchiesi, I apologize for this sudden entrance, but this really couldn't wait," he said when the older woman appeared. He thrust the papal brief into her hand, and she and Sister Chiara read it.

"I will fetch Sister Lucrezia," the abbess said curtly as she handed the letter back to Lippo, then disappeared down a hall.

Lippo forgot his weariness and impatience when Lucrezia stood before him. She was still beautiful and he still longed for her.

"Come, Sister Chiara," the abbess said, and the two of them left the entrance hall. Sister Chiara moved reluctantly, not taking her eyes off Lippo and Lucrezia until she was too far into the convent's dark depths to see them.

Lippo and Lucrezia sat in the nun's parlor, before the fireplace and its dying embers. Lucrezia read the papal brief.

Lippo spoke un-enthusiastically. "So, through my patron's misguided but well-meant efforts, we are married, and Filippino is legitimized."

"And you have come here to 'fetch' me, is that right?" Lucrezia said.

"If you'll come with me, that is," Lippo said, clinging to hope.

"Have you forgotten that I made a solemn, personal vow to re-enter this place, quite apart from my public vows? As far as the Church is concerned, with this piece of paper my vow is removed, but what about me?"

Lippo's voice was very gentle. "Lucrezia, even if you leave now, you have fulfilled your promise. You renewed your nun's vows, gave up your son and resumed the religious life. Isn't the debt paid?"

Lucrezia stood and walked to the parlor window. She looked without seeing at the night shapes in the convent's little garden.

"No. For the life of a child, the debt is never paid." She paused. "But I have missed Filippino. I've cried for him...."

Silence hung in the dim parlor. Still looking out at the garden, Lucrezia said softly, "Yes, I'll go with you."

Lippo felt rivers of tension drain from his limbs as Lucrezia sat down again opposite him. "But why did Cosimo have to arrange for us to be married?" she asked. "I don't want that! Why didn't you simply tell Cosimo that was quite thoughtful, but unnecessary?"

"How could I say that to the man who has helped me so much? To tell Cosimo de'Medici that he should not have done such a generous thing would have been a hideous insult. I had to accept the papal brief, including the part about marriage," Lippo said.

"We both know that you, Filippino and I might live under one roof, but we can never be like most families. I'm resigned to that," Lucrezia said. "So what do we do?"

"We'll let our marriage exist only on paper. That seems to suit us both," Lippo said.

"I suppose that's how it will have to be," Lucrezia said. Suddenly her voice turned passionate. "Oh, Lippo, I want to see my son--now!" She dashed off to collect her prayer book from her cell. Once again, she tossed her veil on the bed. Then she and Lippo left the convent, awakened the woman caring for Filippino, and brought him home.

When they had put the boy to sleep, Lucrezia turned to Lippo.

"When I said I had missed Filippino, well, I missed you, too," she said.

Lippo reached for her. "Criza..." he said, and they fell together, their lips touched, reminding each of their abandoned love. Both felt the reawakening of buried urgings, so they laid themselves on the feather bed, and they spoke no more that night.

And instantly, the gossips of Prato lost their favorite topic. After all, what could be more respectable than a family joined by the Pope? In the house in the Gorellina with Filippino, Lippo and Lucrezia soon felt nearly contented, which was more than either had ever thought possible.

Late in 1461 the Commune of Perugia asked Lippo to evaluate paintings by Benedetto Bonfigli in the chapel of the Commune's palazzo. The evaluation would help to set a fair price for the work.

While Lippo was gone from Prato, the various committees in charge of the choir frescoes continued to grumble about his slowness in completing the job. As years passed, and scaffolding and paint pots and brushes seemed to become permanent fixtures in the choir, more than one person silently wished that the steadfast Fra Giovanni had accepted the commission. But Lippo had to finish the Nativity for the Medici chapel, and in 1463, yet another Medici commission intervened--this time from Lucrezia Tornabuoni de'Medici, wife of Piero.

Lippo had heard that she, not the sickly Piero, did much of the work of running Florence. She was enthusiastic about painting, and had prompted and guided Gozzoli as he created the Medici chapel frescoes. Above all, she was a gifted poet. Her poems reflected her religious devotion, and had an emotional depth and literary quality rare in such writings.

Lippo was shown to the second-floor drawing room of the Medici palazzo, lush with carpets imported from the East. On the plain walls hung religious paintings, and shelves held a terracotta bust of the Madonna and other ornaments of glass and bronze. Two maids sat discreetly across the room, busying themselves with embroidery.

Lucrezia waited at a small desk. Lippo was struck at once by the beauty of her flawless pale skin and brown eyes. She asked him about his progress on the Prato frescoes, and in his marvelling he coughed out a barely coherent response. By the time Lucrezia came to the point of the visit, Lippo was hopelessly charmed.

"The family has built a cell for the Camaldolite hermitage in the Casentino. I want a panel painting to hang in the cell--a panel showing the Madonna adoring the newborn Child. It must be reverent and likely to inspire meditation. Will you do it?"

Lippo almost laughed at what he considered a silly question--he was so captivated by this other Lucrezia that he would have done absolutely anything for her. He wanted very much to make love to her, but for once in his life, he dismissed the idea firmly. He didn't dare to imagine the penalty if he were caught making love to the wife of a Medici, especially such a greatly beloved one as Lucrezia.

"Yes, Monna de'Medici, I'll do it. What exactly do you require?"

Lucrezia handed him a contract listing the planned dimensions of the work, and certain figures that it should contain, such as Sts. Bernard, and John the Baptist as a boy. This final request made Lippo curious.

"Most respected Monna de'Medici, I notice that you would like to see the Baptist portrayed as a boy. Other Medici have made the same request for other works I've done. May I ask why?"

Lucrezia picked up a book from the desk. "I'm not sure about the others, but I have been reading some of the legends of the saints, especially a legend of the last century that describes the Baptist's childhood. It's a charming story, and not written in Latin but in our own language. Let me read some to you."

Lippo fell instantly under the spell of her sweet voice, and wanted to stay for hours just listening to its music. He was quite disappointed when she stopped.

"I won't keep you any longer. I just wanted to show you where I received my inspiration. The rest of the inspiration will have to come from you, Fra Filippo," and she gave him a smile so lovely that Lippo felt as if all his bones had melted. They said goodbye, and somehow, reluctantly, he found the strength to turn and leave the room.

That night, in the bordello, Lippo imagined that the skinny creature servicing him was Lucrezia Tornabuoni de'Medici, that he was holding her close, and that she was returning his ardor.

In the panel, the Virgin's glowing figure, with a high forehead, youthful features and delicate hands, dominated a rocky landscape of gloomy earth tones. Beside her, Lippo made all else distinctly secondary: of God, the Father, Lippo showed only hands in the heavens; he placed St. Bernard deep in a corner, and young John the Baptist hard against the right edge. When he had finished, Lippo wondered whether his fascination with Lucrezia Tornabuoni had crept into the way he had painted the Virgin. It was a fascination never to be revealed, much less fulfilled.

Besides, he had his own Lucrezia, blue-eyed and equally lovely. He didn't know about her restlessness. One day she approached the Ceppo Nuovo, an institution for the poor, founded decades before by the Pratese merchant, Francesco Datini. Lippo had painted the Madonna and Child panel above the Ceppo's courtyard well.

The woman who directed the Ceppo was a tired-looking soul who scanned Lucrezia thoroughly.

"Lucrezia di Francesco Buti," she repeated. "Haven't I heard that name before? Yes! You're the one who left the convent and ran off with that false monk, Lippo Lippi! So, now you have repented. Is that why you're offering yourself here?"

"I repent nothing! Since I was a child, my mother and father told me I had a responsibility to help the poor. They said comfort wasn't an end in itself, but a tool given by God, and anyone who had it must help the less fortunate. The poor need help, and I'm able to give it. If you expect me to express shame and remorse, I'll go elsewhere," Lucrezia said.

"All right, never mind. We certainly need help. Come with me."

Lucrezia learned quickly the hard, ugly facts of poverty. In Prato, as elsewhere, poor relief generally was left to the Church and private charities. Civic authorities sometimes used public money to ease hardship, but not until unemployment and hunger reached dangerous levels. Monasteries fed the poor who came to their gates. Wealthy individuals like Datini, perhaps out of guilt, founded institutions to look after the poor, the sick, foundlings and other unfortunates.

Lucrezia helped feed farm families who came to the Ceppo when a poor harvest threatened them with starvation, or when their fields were ruined by marauding armies.

Her strong, loving arms cuddled the foundlings occasionally left on the Ceppo's doorstep. Most of them were girls, because many families preferred sons to daughters. Sometimes the babies arrived with notes from their parents saying they feared scandal, or simply couldn't afford to feed the infant.

Every day Lucrezia held the hands of the sick---some, their bodies ravaged by malnutrition; others, by infections that spread more easily among the poor in their hovels than the rich in their stone-built houses.

She also looked without flinching, and with infinite compassion, into the searing face of death.

Gradually Lucrezia earned the respect of the institution's other workers. Some of them had dismissed her at first as a delicate do-gooder who wouldn't stay long after her first whiff of poverty. But she endured, and she rejoiced in a feeling of self-worth and usefulness. As in the convent, the beautiful, educated Lucrezia stood out vividly among the miserable, illiterate people she cared for. Perhaps it was not surprising that at least one person was astounded by her decision to work among the poor.

The Funeral of St. Stephen. Among the faces in the group of mourners standing to the right of the bier are believed to be portraits of Lippi and Diamante. The exact portrayals are uncertain.

Chapter 13

Advance then, and with good and favorable
omen, ascend
with high courage even to the peak, so that
wreathed with
laurel you may be seen in your own glory
by those panting in the ascent...
Giovanni Boccaccio, *letter to Jacopo Pizzinghe*,
trans. Mary Martin McLaughlin

L ippo confronted her one day as she was about to leave for the Ceppo.

"Just what are you doing there among all those wretches? You're not going back," he said.

"Not going back? Of course I'm going back--as often as I choose. It's what I *want* to do, can you understand that?" Lucrezia said.

"But, Lucrezia, let others do it! You--you're special, you're different...."

Lucrezia snorted with disgust. "Lippo, you have always looked at me as your pure, celestial Madonna. Well, I'm sick of that! I am not some delicate creature to sit on a shelf, above the mean world. I'm no different from other women, except in your mind."

"What about Filippino? I don't want my son playing in such a place, among orphans and urchins of the street!" Lippo fumed.

"Filippino is just fine! He spends no more time at the Ceppo than he does in your studio. Besides, have you forgotten that you, too, were an orphan? You were lucky to have an aunt to take you in. The children of the Ceppo have nobody." She paused. "You know, I never asked for your help with Filippino. He's as much my son as yours. You'll just have to trust me."

Lippo, for once out of arguments, turned and left the house.

In October of 1463, an exasperated Prato city council sent a committee to Carlo de'Medici, Cosimo's illegitimate son and new head of the parish church, to discuss Lippo's slow progress on the choir frescoes.

"He started the work 11 years ago--it didn't take that long for God to create the world!" they complained. Carlo, reluctant to push Lippo, tried to soothe them.

"This dilatoriness of Lippo's--isn't it to be expected from an artist?" he asked them. "Surely you've heard of how Jacopo della Quercia endlessly delayed work on the Fonte Gaia in Siena. The Commune gave him 20 months to finish it, but he took more than 10 years. And then in Bologna, when he carved the reliefs around the doors of San Petronio--the contract said two years, but when della Quercia died more than 13 years later, the work still wasn't done. So can't we make allowances, especially for a painter of Lippo's ability?"

The committee, unmoved, decided to audit the fresco contract. To their surprise, they learned that Lippo had observed all conditions of the contract, and in fact was still owed 40 florins. They agreed to pay him, but still wanted assurance that he would indeed finish the work soon.   Lippo was an old man, and Carlo's reminder that Jacopo della Quercia had died before finishing his Bologna work weighed heavily on the minds of committee members.

Carlo went to Lippo, determined to win him over with reason.

"Obviously a work so large must take a long time. Such an endeavor cannot be rushed, if it is to meet your high standards," Carlo said evenly.

Lippo looked with the curious eye of a painter at the features of Carlo's swarthy face.   The provost had high cheekbones, deep-set eyes, flaring nostrils and a broad mouth.   He bore little resemblance to Cosimo--- perhaps he more closely resembled his mother, a Circassian slave girl who had lived with Cosimo in Rome while he was manager of the Medici bank branch there many years ago.   Such circumstances of birth were not exceptional.   No one was surprised when Carlo was raised with Cosimo's other sons and given a classical education.

Carlo continued.   "I firmly agree with my father, who said artists of genius were not to be treated as pack mules.   But perhaps, Lippo--perhaps it is time to bring this project to a close."

"You've been more than patient," Lippo replied. "Not many would wait so long without a word of com- plaint.   I'll try to have the work completed by autumn next year."

Carlo had hoped for an earlier completion date, but he agreed.   In gratitude for Carlo's patience and the freedom he had bestowed, Lippo painted the provost's likeness among the mourners at the funeral of St. Stephen.

But Carlo's entreaties came just as the frescoes entered a difficult phase. Lippo had planned an enormous, complicated scene showing King Herod's Banquet, with Salomé dancing, and the head of John the Baptist carried in on a platter. Almost without conscious decision, he lightened the drudgery of the task by giving Salomé Lucrezia's features.

When the piece was finished, he and Diamante stood before it and sighed with relief.

"You spent an awful lot of time on Salomé, and you wouldn't let any of the apprentices work on her," Diamante said. "Is it my imagination, or does her face resemble a certain former nun?"

"What do you mean? The little tart Salomé, resembling a nun? Impossible! And if you mean my Lucrezia, you can see that Salomé is nowhere near as lovely," Lippo protested.

Lippo and his helpers made much progress on the frescoes during the spring and summer of 1464. In August, while seated in their usual tavern, Lippo and Diamante encountered travelers from Florence, who told them about the recent death of Cosimo de'Medici, at age 76.

"Cosimo!" Lippo gasped, and held his head in grief. His words came slowly. "I never cared about the powerful--I saw them all as greedy beasts--that is, all but Cosimo. He believed in me and stood by me. It's a pity he didn't live to see my masterpiece here completed. It wouldn't exist if not for him."

In Florence, in the candlelight of San Lorenzo, Lippo stood silently before Cosimo's body. He remembered the first day he met Cosimo, his furor when Cosimo locked him in his studio, Cosimo's resulting remorse, and the total freedom the man had ever after allowed him. Finally Lippo recalled the commission for the Prato church frescoes--it had been the lift and the challenge he desperately needed after his devastating experience in prison.

As Lippo stood by the coffin, the old man who cleaned the church slowly approached, his head bent toward the floor he was sweeping. He ignored Lippo-- after all, he'd seen many people in the past few days standing as Lippo stood now, paying their respects to Cosimo.

"This man saved me," Lippo said to the man, who didn't respond, but looked up and watched curiously as Lippo turned and left the church. Then the old man shrugged and resumed the gentle whisking of his broom.

Finally, in the late winter of 1465, Lippo ordered the scaffolding removed and the Prato frescoes unveiled. A special High Mass of celebration was held.

Lippo, who seldom attended Mass, reveled in this one, although as usual he paid little attention to the service. Instead he let his eyes roam with loving approval over each detail in the work, and he regarded the singing of the choir as a heavenly chorus justly praising his masterpiece.

Several painters from Florence came to Prato for the Mass and to see the work for themselves. In the nearly 13 years it had taken to complete the frescoes, so many rumors had spread about them that they had assumed almost mythic qualities. The visitors were not disappointed.

"Magnificent!" they proclaimed as they gathered in small groups before the frescoes, struck first by the grandeur and loftiness of the entire work. They loved Lippo's subtle colors, and the great variety of shades he had spread across the scenes. He seemed to have opened up the flat walls to endlessly deep vistas.

On either side of the window, Lippo had painted San Giovanni Gualberto, founder of the Vallombrosan order, and St. Albert, a noted Carmelite. He placed the four Evangelists in the vaulted sections of the roof. The figures were majestic and impressive, but natural.

His fellow painters praised Lippo's composition of the scene of Herod's banquet, on the right wall of the choir. They talked most about the sensual dancing figure of Salomé, both voluptuous and innocent. They prized her high forehead, expressive eyes, and full lips, and the way her hair and gown flew with her whirling dance.

The Florentine poet and expert on rhetoric, Cristoforo Landino, admired the gracefulness of Lippo's figures, especially the two to the right of the banquet scene. They are repulsed by the sundered head of the Baptist, yet unable to take their eyes from it.

Lippo had poured all his artistic power into the climactic and grandiose scene of the Funeral of St. Stephen, on the left wall of the choir. Two rows of columns march into the background, showing Lippo's mastery of perspective. In the foreground, two seated women weep for Stephen, while groups of solemn and cold clergymen gather at each end of his bier. Over them all hangs an air of relentless and sober realism.

Most of all, Lippo's admirers praised the force and vitality of his figures, and Lippo's gift for showing character through faces--in the tenderness of St. John the Baptist's farewell to his parents, the snide indifference of the Pharisees toward St. Stephen, the vicious fury of Stephen's executioners, and the shock of Herod's dinner guests at the sight of the Baptist's severed head.

Lippo's depiction of living people caused a buzz of speculation among the visiting painters. A few recognized Lucrezia as Salomé; all saw Lippo and Diamante among the mourners for St. Stephen. Most of the painters believed that such portraiture would disturb some Pratesi.

Lippo had used live models before, of course--- Lucrezia was the inspiration for that fateful altarpiece in the nuns' chapel, only a short walk from the church. But an altarpiece in a small chapel, hidden from the general public, was one thing--here were living people in an enormous work that many Pratesi were bound to see over and over again. However, the painters doubted that the pious Pratesi would object to the portrait of their provost, Carlo.

The directors of the four committees who super-vised the project gathered around Lippo in the choir.

"We are immensely pleased with your work, Fra Filippo."

"The frescoes are stunningly beautiful and will give us great joy for all time."

"It's at least as good as anything in Florence. You have honored us."

"Please forgive the false accusations that were made, Fra Filippo. Every time you were accused of bad faith or of spending too much on the frescoes, the charges proved unjustified."

Lippo bathed proudly in glory and vindication, and carried this acclaim with him forever like a shield.

It was natural that a boy would take up his father's profession, and Filippino had always played in his father's studio. He had come to know the cool feel of a paintbrush in his hands, the smell of each pigment, the bustle of creative people at work. Now that Filippino was seven, he was old enough to become an apprentice. With painting in common, father and son finally began to draw close to each other. Everyone congratulated Lippo on his courteous, fine-looking boy.

"My son is everything I'm not," Lippo told Diamante. "Polite, friendly, never envious, rarely cranky or selfish, never crude. He's really much more like his mother than like me. What did I do to deserve such a good son?"

On a day in early spring, Lippo, Lucrezia and Filippino walked together beyond Prato's walls, into the hills, wandering slowly across the swaying meadows, hearing the larks' serenade.

Suddenly Lippo groaned softly and sat down on a rock. Filippino, unaware, ran ahead in pursuit of a butterfly.

"What is it?" Lucrezia asked Lippo fearfully.

"It's nothing," Lippo said, forcing himself to smile.

Lucrezia sat beside him. "I know you were imprisoned years ago, Lippo, and I know what can happen in those places. Why don't you tell me about it?"

"No."

"Why not?" she demanded.

"There are some things a man can't say." He groaned again.

"You mean you can't tell me because I'm a woman?"

"No, it's not that."

Lucrezia felt rage rising within her. All at once she was quite tired of Lippo, his self-centeredness, and his turbulent ways. She muttered, "I'll bet you've told some whore or other!"

Then she stood up and ran off after Filippino. Lippo watched them as they walked away.

The Coronation of the Virgin, in Spoleto Cathedral. This fresco fills the vault over the main altar.

woman of the many he had known now sat opposite him every day, yet he dared not touch her!

By the first of May, 1456, when Lucrezia had been posing for four weeks, the desire Lippo had felt growing all along tore at him undeniably. He paused in his painting and glanced at the elderly chaperon. Sister Francesca had fallen asleep in her chair. He seized the chance.

"Lucrezia--" he breathed, then stopped, his brush in midair.

She looked into his face with those azure eyes--- the eyes that had fired Lippo's imagination the first time he saw her in the chapel. He could not stop his index finger from poking nervously toward the studio floor. With characteristic impulsiveness, Lippo set down his brush and charged on.

"Lucrezia, I must see you. Tonight. Everyone in Prato will be occupied with the Feast, trying to see how much they can eat and drink while venerating the Virgin. You can leave the convent and not be missed. I'll wait for you after dark beyond the southern wall, in the cypress grove past the barley field."

Lucrezia's face flashed in surprise and anger.

"What are you saying?" she replied, in a strained whisper, although she knew.

Chapter 14

Yea, let me praise my lady whom I love,
Likening her unto the lily and rose:
Brighter than morning star her visage glows;
She is beneath even as her Saint above.

Guido Guinizelli,
trans. Dante Gabriele Rossetti

Lippo had always disliked Giovanni de'Medici, Cosimo's second son, even before the time Cosimo had sent Giovanni to the Florentine studio to pressure Lippo into diligence. Lippo found Giovanni's obesity offensive. But Giovanni was a good judge of painting, so when he had commissioned a small panel shortly before his death in 1463, Lippo had accepted gladly. The Madonna and Child was to decorate one of the Medici villas.

However, Lippo was too busy then with the Prato church frescos and the panel for Lucrezia Tornabuoni. When Giovanni died, throwing the commission into doubt, Lippo had made no progress on it beyond ordering the wooden panel and having the apprentices prepare it. But Giovanni's widow said she wanted the panel completed, and she paid Lippo an advance for the materials.

When it was time to begin preliminary sketches, he turned to Lucrezia. They were sitting at the table, watching the last of the day's firewood smoulder, before going to bed. "You must model for me! No one makes a finer Madonna."

Lucrezia looked at Lippo with exasperation.

"Lippo, I am 32 years old. I am much too old to portray the virginal Madonna."

"Too old! *Santo Cielo*! You are still beautiful, and you could never be too old to model for me!" Lippo replied.

"There you go again--thinking of me as your ever-blooming, innocent young Madonna. This is really getting tiresome. I suggest you find yourself a model who truly is fresh and sweet and young," Lucrezia said.

Lippo paused, then spoke in a rare voice, low and firm.

"Lucrezia, it doesn't really matter who my model is. All my Madonnas will always be you."

Lucrezia pulled her shawl tighter around her shoulders. "There's another reason I can't model for you. I'll be having a baby in December." Lippo's eyes widened a moment, then he lifted Lucrezia off her chair and embraced her.

"Ah, Lucrezia! Do you feel tired?"

"A little," Lucrezia said. There was no point in telling Lippo that her tension was due to her dread of the rigors of childbirth, which would be worse at her age, and the drudgery of infant care that would follow. And it saddened her to realize that Lippo, at age 59, was an old man and probably would not see this child grow up.

"You're certainly handling this better than you handled the thought of Filippino's coming," Lucrezia said.

"What a fool I was then, to have been so afraid," Lippo said. "Filippino has made me happy--more than I deserve--and so will this little one."

Lippo became solicitous almost to the point of comedy--suddenly he would scarcely let Lucrezia open a door. Lucrezia welcomed this as a distraction from her sorrows.

For the figures in his Madonna panel, Lippo applied the color in bold strokes. In the background he placed an intricate landscape of hedgerows and cliffs. He painted the Madonna without using a model, and as he had predicted, she looked much like Lucrezia years before, when Lippo first knew he deeply desired her.

Lippo considered it the most attractive small panel he had ever done. He personally presented it to Giovanni's widow, Ginevra degli Albizzi, who studied the figures closely.

"She's so real, Fra Lippo--I think if I touched your Madonna's cheek, I would feel flesh instead of paint. She looks like a beautiful Florentine girl I might see in church, or dancing in the Mayfest. But then Our Lady, too, was an ordinary girl, called to an extraordinary destiny. And you have made her son look more like a living baby than like a Savior."

"I hope that doesn't displease you, Monna de'Medici," Lippo said.

"Not at all! I'm very happy with this work. The most intriguing figure is that smiling angel. He looks more interested in mischief than in the spiritual," Ginevra said.

"And many would say, so am I," Lippo said. "Your esteemed late father-in-law, may his soul rest, said every painter paints himself. I never understood what he meant by that. Now, maybe I do. Maybe I am that angel."

Not all of Ginevra degli Albizzi's contemporaries appreciated the irreverence of that angel. Some upright citizens still hadn't excused Lucrezia's flight from the convent and her elopement, and they considered it willful sacrilege for Lippo to paint a Madonna that resembled her, even if they were married now. To also paint an angel with insufficient awe for the Madonna was just too much. Lippo was not offended by these snubs--as always, he took a certain pride in the affront.

The painting showed clearly how much Lippo's style had changed since the middle of the century. The realism he had learned from Masaccio, and the emotion he had learned from Donatello, now gave way to an idealized sweetness and a poetic quality in all his Nativities and Madonna and Child panels. He wasn't sure how the change originated. The work of Domenico Veneziano and other fellow painters showed the same tendency, but had they influenced Lippo, or he them? Lucrezia's fairness had certainly inspired him, but he had sought to capture female beauty in his work even before he met her. Lippo could only be sure of passing the new style on to his outstanding pupil, Botticelli.

While Lippo worked in the studio one wet day in December 1465, a neighbor of Lucrezia's brought word that she soon would give birth. This time Lippo walked as fast as his stocky legs allowed. To his relief, the baby's cries were already filling the small house when he arrived.

Lucrezia was tired but well. After a few minutes, Lucrezia's cousin carried out to him a red-faced, wrinkled girl that Lucrezia had named Alessandra.

"Not exactly the image of her beautiful mother," Lippo said wryly, but he was thoroughly happy. As with Filippino, he delighted in the sight of the baby feeding at Lucrezia's superb ivory breast, bathed in candlelight.

The many years Lippo spent on the Prato frescoes, and his intemperance, finally began to drag him down. He suffered more often from the pains that were the legacy of the rack. As a youth he could walk across Florence in 20 minutes; now the same distance took him much longer, and the still-beautiful city enchanted him far less. He continued to worship Eros, but less frequently and with far less gusto. Death ruled constantly in his plague-ridden, violent land, yet Lippo had always pictured his life as stretching away endlessly before him. Now, suddenly, he could see a firm horizon.

Encounters with women were rarer but more significant. He wanted from them not just carnal satisfaction, but comfort and solace, and he thought about their pleasure as much as his own.

His work offered small satisfaction. He accepted fewer commissions and took more time than ever to finish them. With the Prato frescoes complete, he worked on panels, and a burden he had not felt since the monastery now overcame him: boredom. After the grand challenge of the Prato frescoes, panel pictures no longer held his interest. They were worthy commissions, but he handled them without the spark he had known in his youth. He needed the grandiose once more, a work that told a sweeping tale, but he was old, and losing strength.

In the previous year, as death closed in on Cosimo de'Medici, he had instructed his son and heir, Piero, to always treat Lippo as someone exceptional--a painter who deserved more than the customary respect. In January 1466, Piero summoned Lippo to Florence.

Lippo was shown into Piero's lavishly decorated study, and Piero greeted him courteously. Piero suffered severely from gout, and the Medici bad skin that afflicted his otherwise handsome, full-jawed face. Some people complained of a coldness in his manner, and Lippo had never forgotten Piero's refusal to help him with his destitute nieces years before. After exchanging polite information about the health of their wives and children, Piero explained why he had summoned Lippo.

"The Commune of Spoleto would like to have frescoes painted on the walls behind the main altar of the cathedral there. They are very impressed with your fine work at Prato, and asked if you would do the same for them," Piero said.

Spoleto! Lippo desperately wanted such a commission, but Spoleto was 100 miles away, over difficult roads. He was 60 years old--if he went to Spoleto, he might never see Lucrezia or Florence again. Still....

The chance to work once again in the monumental manner won out. He accepted the offer.

The light of Umbria veils the poplar-studded hills and valleys with a bluish haze, so different from the clear, sharp light of Tuscany. In April 1466, Lippo, Diamante, and 9-year-old Filippino rode their mules into this haze, turning southeast off the ancient Via Cassia at Chiusi and onto rugged, unwelcoming cart paths. Three days after leaving Florence, they arrived in austere but pretty Spoleto, an old Roman colony spread out on a hillside.

A large committee in charge of the cathedral's decoration warmly greeted Lippo's group. The three were taken to an inn for a lavish supper. After eating, Lippo excused himself so he could get a look at the cathedral before night fell.

The cathedral stood on a hill where tradition said a temple to Helios had once stood. On the piazza before it, children played on the paving stones in the soft evening light. Water gushed out from a wall on the right, into a Roman sarcophagus. A massive, unadorned square bell tower stood to the left of the cathedral's charming facade. Lippo admired a Byzantine mosaic on the upper part, showing the Redeemer with the Virgin and St. John.

Lippo, Diamante and Filippino spent several days studying the shape of the cathedral's apse and roughly composing the frescoes. The cathedral was dedicated to the Virgin, and the frescoes would depict the Annunciation, the Nativity, the Virgin's death and, for the huge vault above the altar, her Coronation. It was ambitious and Lippo was eager to begin, confident that he could recapture the glory of Prato.

But, as at Prato, several things delayed the start of the work. The surface of the apse needed major repairs. The work proceeded slowly due to unusually intense heat that spring and summer that sapped the energy of Lippo's workmen.

It was late autumn when the resurfacing was finished and Lippo, Filippino and Diamante returned to Prato. Lippo had one last panel painting to finish: the Presentation of the Infant Christ in the Temple, commissioned by the Servite Fathers. He also had to straighten out some business matters, and hire assistants for the Spoleto frescoes.

Lippo spent an unusual number of hours in his studio that winter, drawing and re-drawing detailed plans for the frescoes, striving for perfection.

"What is the problem with this project?" Filippino asked Lippo one day, after watching his father toss aside yet another sketch with a grunt of frustration.

Lippo slumped back in his chair. "This project has to be special. I'm so old. Let's face it--I won't do another project this large."

Filippino stood behind his father's chair and put his arms around Lippo's neck. Such gestures from his son had always made Lippo uncomfortable, but for once he didn't squirm.

A few days later, Lippo, Filippino and Diamante went to Florence after hearing about the death of the sculptor Donatello.

The city dressed itself in grief, in grim veils of mourning cloth. Workshops and banks closed early. In the damp chill of December, every architect, sculptor and painter in Florence, along with thousands of other citizens, followed Donatello's funeral procession to San Lorenzo, where he was buried in the crypt near Cosimo, his friend and patron.

"Why, Papà? Why all this for Donatello? Burial next to Cosimo, and I heard the Medici paid for the funeral," Filippino asked as he left San Lorenzo with his father and Diamante after the ceremonies.

"It's important that you know, my Filippino. No one in Florence had more influence on our work, whether sculpture or painting. Donatello did the first freestanding bronze nude since ancient times. Now, the ancients wanted only to portray perfection of form. Donatello said, yes, form must be perfect, but that's not enough--he demanded that form also convey some message of the mind," Lippo said.

"Study his statue of St. George at Orsanmichele," Diamante said. "It expresses the beauty of youth, and courage. And his bronze David in the Medici courtyard is so natural, you would think it was modeled directly on the human form. These show what a genius Donatello was."

"And he didn't care about money. He put what he earned into a wicker basket in his studio, and all his apprentices and friends could help themselves to whatever they needed. And such a wit," Lippo said, then sighed. "He was eighty-one years old. He was just about the last of us. Brunelleschi, Ghiberti, Fra Giovanni...we Florentine disciples of Masaccio are all gone now."

"Not quite, Papà. You're still here," Filippino said.

"Yes, but I'm old. And I'm leaving Florence, maybe for good. It's time for others to carry on--Botticelli, Della Francesca, Gozzoli, Verrocchio, and you, my son."

The next day Lippo found himself wandering the neighborhood of his youth--Via dell'Ardiglione and the orchard behind it where he played, and the little market square where he used to filch fruit. He stopped on the piazza in front of the Carmelite church for a while, then walked up the steps and inside.

It was cool and peaceful, as he remembered. Someone was practicing the organ. Lippo went straight to the chapel he had known as the Brancacci.

Now it was called the Chapel of Our Lady of the People, after a panel painting of the Virgin that the Carmelites had placed over the altar. The Brancacci family had suffered dishonor by opposing the Medici; Felice Brancacci had been exiled in 1436 and declared a rebel. To avoid the embarrassment and possible danger of association with such a family, the Carmelites not only renamed the chapel, but obliterated portraits of everyone related to the Brancacci that Masaccio had painted in the scene of the Raising of the Son of Theophilus.

For painters, the chapel remained a place of pilgrimage. Dozens had visited over the years to admire Masaccio's work. Lippo wondered what would have happened to him if Masaccio had never come to the Carmelite church. By what slender threads a man's life can hang!

The unfinished, mutilated state of the chapel walls depressed him, and he left quickly.

In mid-March of 1467, when all the Prato chores were done, and the designs for the Spoleto frescoes completed, Lippo said goodbye to Lucrezia. They chatted amiably about Lippo's plans for the frescoes, and Filippino's happiness about his first major project as an apprentice. While they talked, little Alessandra ran in and out of the room, babbling cheerfully.

"This project won't take as long as the Prato frescoes, but it could be about two years," Lippo said. Lucrezia understood that he was trying to prepare her for a long separation.

Finally Lippo scooped up the laughing Alessandra and held her close, wanting to memorize the sweet scent of her skin. "*Addio, cara,*" he said, and kissed her fat cheek. He set her back down on the floor.

Lippo put his arms around Lucrezia and looked into her exquisite blue eyes. He loosened her hair, grown once again past her breasts into a billowing yellow stream. They began to kiss gently, then, as if washed by a single wave, both pressed their lips and bodies closer, breathlessly, achingly.

Then they both whispered *addio*, and he was gone.

A few hours later, Lucrezia's cousin Caterina arrived in Prato for a visit.

"Cati! Lippo just said goodbye. He'll be leaving for Spoleto soon, and I don't expect to see him for a while," Lucrezia told her cousin as the women settled in the parlor.

"Remember when you first left the convent?" Caterina asked.

"Remember! I'll never forget it. I felt like a caged bird set free. And I was so relieved to have finally--uh, to have finally escaped a nun's fate," Lucrezia said delicately.

Caterina laughed. "You always put things so correctly. That's a tribute to your father for giving you an education," she said. "If I remember right, when you eloped, we said we wouldn't discuss it again. And maybe we wouldn't have, and you never would have seen Lippo again, if it weren't for Filippino," Caterina said.

"That's probably true. Knowing Lippo has certainly made things unconventional, but not entirely unpleasant," Lucrezia said. "Where would I be now if he hadn't desired me? Still dying slowly in the convent of Santa Margherita?"

"No. You would have found another way out," her cousin said.

"Maybe, but I wouldn't have Filippino and Alessandra now, and I can't imagine life without them. Yes, Cati, Lippo is a rogue, and that makes me angry, but I couldn't change him. I managed. And he does love his children."

Lippo's group stopped in Florence on the way to Spoleto, and Lippo went to the Wren to say goodbye to his tavern friends.

The Wren itself hadn't changed much since Lippo first set foot in it, in those heady, vigorous years of his youth. There were the same old battered wooden tables and benches, the smell from the oil lamps, the raunchy banter of friends. But the people of the Wren had changed--Paola the barmaid had long since married and left, Matteo, the coppersmith, had died, and others had simply drifted away.

"Well, I must be off," Lippo said, draining his cup, after he and his companions had emptied some jugs of wine. Some of his friends chuckled, knowing that the bordello was Lippo's usual stop after leaving the tavern.

"I'll be leaving for Spoleto in a few days. The work will take several months, so, if I'm not back soon, be sure and drink to me. *Addio*," he said. As he turned and left, his friends called after him: "Goodbye, you old lecher! Of course we'll drink to you--every chance we get! *Arrivederci*, you naughty bastard!"

"Well, that was strange," Luca, the tailor, said when things had quieted down.

"Strange? What do you mean?" his friends asked.

"Since when did Lippo ever take the time to say goodbye? He usually just dashes off with barely a word, as soon as the mood strikes. Why not this time?"

The Annunciation, in Spoleto Cathedral. Again the Madonna's features are believed to resemble Lucrezia Buti's.

Chapter 15

Perch'i' no spero di tornar giammai,
ballatetta, in Toscana,
va tu, leggera e piana,
dritt'a la donna mia,
che per sua cortesia
ti farà molto onore.

Since I have no hope of returning ever,
little ballad, to Tuscany,
go, lightly and softly,
direct to my lady,
who, in her courtesy,
will do you much honor.

Guido Cavalcanti, author's translation

L ippo was happy to return to Spoleto, accompanied by Filippino, Diamante, several apprentices, and mules loaded with supplies. They stopped in the main square to ask about the house that the cathedral committee had promised them. Lippo had barely dismounted when he noticed two women, one very old and one young, standing by the well. The younger woman wore a black veil that suddenly, unaccountably, slipped off her head. Before replacing it, she looked at Lippo boldly with curious black eyes. Then both women disappeared together down a side street. Lippo asked one of the apprentices to find out who the younger woman was.

After several days of sleuthing, the faithful apprentice made his report. The darkly beautiful woman had the ironic name of Bianca--Bianca Landrini de'Celani, daughter of a wealthy merchant. She was 20 years old, but a widow, her husband having died two years before in a hunting accident.

"And she has several older brothers who I'm told can be rather brutish," the apprentice said to Lippo urgently.

Lippo laughed and placed a hand on the boy's shoulder. "Don't look so worried! Come on, we have a lot of work to do." But even as he concentrated on the frescoes, Lippo's thoughts returned often to the dark Bianca.

That evening he wandered alone to the main square of the town. It was filled with people enjoying their daily walk in the mild air. Lippo saw Bianca across the square, standing with her maid. He waited until the maid turned away from Bianca to join a circle of women. Then he strolled to within a few steps of her. Their eyes met briefly.

"I hope you find our Spoletan evenings pleasant," Bianca said, looking away from him.

"Indeed, I do," Lippo answered, just as casually, despite his impatience with such talk.

"And what are the evenings like in Prato?" Bianca asked, her black eyes still looking everywhere but at Lippo.

"So you know where I've been working the past several years," Lippo said.

"Oh, I know a *great deal* about you," Bianca said. She saw that her maid's conversation was breaking up, and that the woman would soon be glued to her side once again.

She whispered to Lippo hurriedly: "Palazzo Landrini. Use the side stairs. Knock twice. At midnight." Then her maid, who had not noticed Lippo and had heard nothing, took her by the arm, and they walked off across the square.

Lippo could hardly eat the stew Filippino had prepared in their small house near the cathedral. He slept briefly, lightly, then headed out into the moonlit night when the cathedral bell tolled 12 times.

The city was silent as death, and not one window glowed with candlelight. Palazzo Landrini loomed over the smaller houses of the street.

Although raging with eagerness, Lippo walked slowly up the side stairs, not wanting to make noise. He knocked twice, and Bianca answered almost immediately.

He stepped inside, into blackness. Bianca led him by the arm down a short corridor and into a small bedroom.

Bianca let her brocade robe drop from her shoulders, and stood naked in the moonlight shining through a high window. Lippo couldn't have composed the scene better if he were sitting in his studio, brush in hand. The light formed a halo around her hair, fallen in a fragrant black sheen over the marvelous curves of her breasts. Lippo took in her silhouette: a tiny waist, full hips, gracefully shaped legs.... But he had only a moment to savor the sight, before Bianca reached out and pulled him close. The intensity of her kisses overwhelmed him. He let her lead him to the bed, where he laid back as she moved her lips over his hairless chest and across his belly.

Lippo had never known such a bold woman. He was an old man, and he feared being unable to pleàse her. But Bianca prodded him patiently, and at last shifted above him and took him inside her, until both struggled to keep from screaming with pleasure.

Much later, still tangled together, they spoke their first words of the night.

"So you are Fra Filippo Lippi, former monk, for years now painter extraordinaire and favorite of the Medici," Bianca said.

Bianca's complete lack of inhibition fascinated Lippo. "Yes, I suppose that sums me up neatly," he said. "My reputation must have arrived in Spoleto before I did."

"Almost," Bianca said with a chuckle.

"But why did you choose me, dear Bianca? I'm old. You could have any young man in Spoleto."

"And I don't want any of them. The young men of Spoleto are big of bone but small of brain. I heard about you years ago, from friends of my father who had lived in Prato. A painter, an ardent lover, and a monk! I was intrigued. I vowed if I ever had a chance, I would come to know such a remarkable man. When I heard you had accepted the cathedral fresco commission, I knew our time was near."

They kissed again, passionately, and Lippo let himself get blissfully lost in Bianca's rose-scented skin, soft as down.

When he descended the stairs later, Lippo thought he heard a rustle of clothing and quick footsteps in the nearby courtyard of the palazzo. But though he looked carefully, he saw no one, and returned home with his light mood unbroken.

During the next several months Lippo and Bianca met in the small room frequently. And each evening they appeared to ignore each other when they passed in the square. Filippino noticed his father's nocturnal ramblings, but said nothing.

Occasionally after leaving Bianca, Lippo would sense unfriendly eyes watching him, perhaps silent feet following as he walked home. One night he thought he glimpsed Alfredo, one of Bianca's brothers, watching as he left the palazzo. But the figure disappeared before Lippo could confront him. He never mentioned his unease to anyone.

Next to Bianca, Lippo's greatest joy came from teaching Filippino. The boy learned quickly, and showed genuine skill. Lippo let him paint bits of the background areas and architectural details of the frescoes. "Now, do it this way," Lippo said, and Filippino followed, in careful emulation.

A sudden, intense wave of nausea hit Lippo one morning the following spring. He lay in bed for one day, then, feeling stronger, returned to the cathedral, eager to continue the Coronation of the Virgin fresco that would dominate the altar.

He worked with a desperation he had never felt before. He cursed the body that now so frequently failed him: if it wasn't the lingering pain of the rack in his limbs or organs, it was simple fatigue, forcing him to leave much of the painting to his helpers. He wanted desperately to finish the frescoes before...no, for Lippo there was no thought beyond the end of this project.

But the Coronation of the Virgin, the first part he finished, did not reflect Lippo's visions for it. Indeed, Diamante noted sadly that the fresco didn't approach the brilliance of those at Prato. The wavy rays of the sun, and the bluish green sea on which the Virgin seemed to float, gave the whole scene a mystical look, like Lippo's recent Nativities. Although the ranks of dancing angels brought the work Lippo's characteristic touch of vivacity and joy, it contained little of the vigor and drama of Herod's Banquet. Diamante wondered whether the mystical look of the Umbrian countryside, as well as old age, had influenced his friend.

He knew the inferiority of the Coronation was not all Lippo's fault--because of Lippo's illness, Diamante himself had painted several key parts of the fresco, including the faces of the Virgin and the Lord. He had long ago realized that his talent did not equal Lippo's.

A few months after finishing the Coronation Lippo took sick again, this time with a raging fever. He drifted in and out of consciousness, mumbling words that the doctor and Filippino could not understand.

"Criza!" he would sometimes whisper, sometimes shout. "Are you there? You left the convent! Don't go back! Frate Jacopo's there--he'll be angry!"

Finally the fever broke, and after six weeks of illness and slow recovery, Lippo returned to the frescoes, and to Bianca's arms.

She remained in Lippo's eyes as charming and as irresistible as on their first night of love. But one night, with her, his body failed him in yet another way, for him the worst way possible, and his humiliation was such that he never went to Palazzo Landrini again.

Diamante nearly forgot his disappointment in the Coronation when he saw what Lippo accomplished in the Annunciation scene. Lippo claimed once again the mastery he had shown at Prato, in the suppleness of the Virgin's and the Angel's bodies and clothes, graceful and flowing, and in the softness of their gestures. The delicate and genteel features of the Virgin's face revealed the woman always inside Lippo--the Madonna of the smiling angel, Salomé, the Bartolini Madonna, Lucrezia.

On an early October day in 1469 Lippo concentrated on the Death of the Virgin, the final unfinished section of the fresco series. It resembled his Death of St. Jerome and the Funeral of St. Stephen, but lacked their grandioseness and truth. The scene was set in a sad, dull landscape, where an empty tomb waited in the background. Above the Virgin's deathbed he painted an image of her rising to heaven while bestowing the Holy Belt on St. Thomas.

The work sent his thoughts hurtling back to Lucrezia. She had modeled for his altarpiece of the Madonna of the Holy Belt--they had eloped on the day Prato venerated the relic--*Criza mia! Why did I leave you for this cold, distant town?*

He stared at the mourners around the Virgin's deathbed, whose faces seemed to mock his anguish with an almost frigid indifference. The striking characterizations so highly praised in the Prato frescoes were gone. He had managed only to capture Death perfectly in the thin, lifeless features of the Virgin's face.

Among the Apostles gathered at the left side of the scene, the halo on one figure wasn't quite right. As Lippo reached up with his paintbrush, a stabbing pain shot through his abdomen, and he drew the brush back. He gritted his teeth and tried desperately again to touch his brush to the damp wall--*almost there--got to--finish---*but the pain doubled him over, and he collapsed on the scaffolding.

Diamante and the others carried him home. Lippo protested that he was all right, even as his body twisted in torment. Filippino ran for a doctor.

Lippo slid once again into delirium. "Abdul Maumen...in the Barbary...it was all true...Lucrezia knows...."

The doctor shook his head and gave Filippino no words of comfort.

Suddenly, in the darkest hour of that night, Lippo shrieked, "Alfredo!" Filippino had heard of Bianca's rough brothers, but did not know their names.

"*Papà, Papà*, I'm here," Filippino said with a sob. And Lippo looked at his son in the darkness with infinite sadness.

Then he tossed his head back on the pillow. "Criza..." he said softly, and his hand went limp in Filippino's.

The boy curled up on the edge of the bed, laid his head on his dead father's chest, and waited for dawn.

Lippo's funeral took place in the cathedral of Spoleto, before his unfinished frescoes. In a few sad weeks Diamante, Filippino and the apprentices finished them, then returned to Prato.

Soon after, Filippino left for Florence to enter Botticelli's workshop. They were much alike--both sensitive, and strongly attracted to all that was beautiful. They became good friends and shared many memories of Lippo.

Lucrezia remained in the Prato house on the Gorellina, turning down her cousin's invitation to live with her in Florence. She wanted to stay where she had met and loved Lippo and raised their children. Filippino supported her with his painting. When Alessandra was 17 she married a printer and set up housekeeping in Prato.

In 1484 Filippino received the commission to complete the frescoes in the former Brancacci chapel of the Carmelite church, where his father had studied painting under Masaccio so many years before.

It was a haunting experience, for the very air of the church seemed to contain the memory of Lippo. Filippino knew his father had not been happy in the monastery, and the echoes he heard were anxious indeed....

But the moment he stepped into the chapel, his sense of his father's presence brightened. Turning around, he often expected to see a stocky man in monk's robes, and to hear him say, "Now, do it this way...."

Lorenzo de'Medici, son of Piero, had taken control of Medici affairs after his father died. He went to Spoleto to bring Lippo's body back to Florence for burial. Lorenzo knew well the esteem that his grandfather had held for Lippo, and as a child had met the painter once.

But the Spoletani refused to let the painter go. They argued that Florence had more than its share of illustrious people buried within its walls, and Spoleto had almost none, so Florence could do without this one.

The Spoletani did allow Lorenzo to build a tomb for Lippo within the cathedral, and Lorenzo commissioned Filippino to design it. Now, in 1488, Filippino watched the monument take shape.

He surveyed the skulls and gargoyle faces, the flowers and birds carved in the gray marble. *Motley, just like Papà*, he thought. Prominent amid the marble in Filippino's design for the tomb was a bust of his father, portrayed as the monk he had never truly been.

One index finger pointed downward, a gesture Lippo had painted on his self-portrait in the Death of the Virgin fresco in this same cathedral of Spoleto.

As he watched the sculptors complete his father's tomb, Filippino marveled at the cycle of birth, life and death, and all the smaller circles that whirled within each year, and how they spun apart only to link themselves together later in strange, unpredictable patterns.

When the sculptors left for their midday break, the rector of the cathedral walked in. He was curious about the man on whose tomb Filippino lavished so much attention.

"Tell me about your father," the rector said.

"He was a scoundrel," Filippino began. "He was unreliable, a drunkard, and he knew far too many women."

The rector was surprised, but said nothing.

"He was also a first-rate painter. Maybe that made up for everything else, I don't know." Filippino paused thoughtfully, then grinned. "Come on, let's get some air," he said lightly. "*Papà* would hoot at such gloomy talk."

Epilogue

F ra Filippo Lippi's body found no more rest in death than it did in his hectic life. His remains disappeared from his tomb in the cathedral of Spoleto during restorations in the sixteenth century, and their current whereabouts remain a mystery.

The Death of the Virgin, in Spoleto Cathedral. Lippo is believed to be the monk in a black cap and white cloak pictured at right, standing behind the angel who holds a white candle.

Bibliography

Anderson, A.J., *The Romance of Fra Filippo Lippi.* Stanley Paul & Co., London, 1909.

Antal, Frederick, *Florentine Painting and its Social Background.* Kegan Paul, London, 1947.

Baldini, Umberto, *The Brancacci Chapel.* Translated by Lysa Hochroth. Harry N. Abrams, Inc., New York, 1992.

Bargellini, Piero, *La città di Firenze.* Bonechi Editore, Florence, 1979.

Bargellini, Piero, *Via Larga.* Vallecchi Editore, Florence, 1940.

Baxandall, Michael, *Painting and Experience in 15th Century Italy.* Clarendon Press, Oxford, 1972.

Bec, Christian, *Cultura e società a Firenze nell'età della Rinascenza.* Salerno Editrice, Rome.

Beck, James, *Italian Renaissance Painting.* Harper & Row, New York, 1981.

Berenson, Bernard, *Italian Painters of the Renaissance.* Phaidon Press, New York, 1952.

Berenson, Bernard, *The Florentine Painters of the Renaissance.* G.P. Putnam's Sons, New York, 1909.

Biagi, Guido, *Men and Manners of old Florence.* T. Fisher Unwin, London, 1908.

Boorstin, Daniel J., *The Creators, A History of Heroes of the Imagination*. Random House, New York, 1992.

Borsook, Eve, *The Companion Guide to Florence*. Harper & Row, New York, 1966.

Borsook, Eve, *Fra Filippo Lippi and the Murals for Prato Cathedral*. Mitteilungen des Kunsthistorischen Institutes in Florenz, Band 19, Heft 1, 1975.

Boskovits, Miklós, *Fra Filippo Lippi, i Carmelitani e il Rinascimento*. Arte Cristiana, no. 715, July-Aug. 1986, pp. 235-252.

Boskovits, Miklós, *Tuscan Paintings of the Early Renaissance*. Translated by Eva Rácz. Taplinger Publishing Co., New York, 1968.

Burkhardt, Jacob, *The Civilization of the Renaissance in Italy*. Phaidon Press, New York, 1945.

Chamberlin, E. R., *Everyday Life in Renaissance Times*. G.P. Putnams Sons, New York, 1969.

Chandler, Tertius, and Fox, Gerald, *3,000 Years of Urban Growth*. Academic Press, New York and London, 1974.

Chastel, André, *Italian Art*. Faber & Faber, London, 1963.

Cole, Bruce, *The Renaissance Artist at Work, from Pisano to Titian*. Harper & Row, New York, 1983.

Collison-Morley, L., *The Early Medici*. George Routledge & Sons Ltd., London, 1935.

A Concise Encyclopedia of the Italian Renaissance. Edited by J.R. Hale, Oxford University Press, New York and Toronto, 1981.

Cronin, Vincent, *The Florentine Renaissance*. Collins, London, 1967.

Durant, Will, *The Renaissance*. Simon & Schuster, New York, 1953.

Encyclopedia Americana. Vol. 17, 1981.

Encyclopedia Britannica. Vol. 14, 1973.

Encyclopedia Britannica Macropedia. Vol. 10, 1974.

Encyclopedia Britannica Micropedia. Philip W. Goetz, Ed. in chief. Vol. 9. Chicago, 1985.

Fadalti, P. Gherardo, *Fra Filippo Lippi*. Roseti del Carmelo. Florence, 1969.

Farrington, Margaret Vere, *Fra Lippo Lippi--A Romance*. G.P. Putnam's Sons, New York, 1899.

Fausti, Luigi, *Le pitture di Fra Filippo nel Duomo di Spoleto*. Arti Grafiche Panetto e Petrelli, Spoleto, 1970.

Fleming, William, *Arts and Ideas*. Holt, Rinehart and Winston Inc., New York, 1968.

Fossi, Gloria, *Filippo Lippi*. Translated by Lisa Pelletti Clark. SCALA Istituto Fotografico Editoriale S.p.A., Florence, 1989.

Gail, Marzieh, *Life in the Renaissance*. Random House, New York, 1969.

Gardner, Edmund G., *Florence and its Story*. J.M. Dent & Sons Ltd., London, revised 1953.

Gaye, Giovanni, *Carteggio inedito d'artisti dei secoli XIV, XV, XVI*. Giuseppe Molini, Florence, 1839, reprinted Turin, 1961.

Goodenough, Simon, *The Renaissance--The Living Past*. Arco Publishing Inc., New York, 1979.

Gould, C.H.M., *Early Renaissance - 15th Cent. Italian Painting*. 1965.

Hale, John R., and editors of Time-Life Books. *Renaissance*. New York, 1965.

Hale, Sheila, *The American Express Pocket Guide to Florence and Tuscany*. Prentice Hall Press, New York, 1983.

Hay, Denys, *The Italian Renaissance and its Historical Background*. Cambridge University Press, 1961.

Hay, Denys, and Law, John, *Italy in the Age of the Renaissance, 1380-1530*. Longman, London, 1989.

Heydenreich, Ludwig H., *Il primo Rinascimento*. Translated from French by Marcello Lenzini. Rizzoli Editore, Milan, 1979.

Hibbert, Christopher, *The Rise and Fall of the House of Medici*. Penguin Books, London, 1979.

Hohenberg, Paul M., and Lees, Lynn Hollen, *The Making of Urban Europe 1000-1950*. Harvard University Press, Cambridge, 1985.

The Horizon Book of the Renaissance. Editors of Horizon magazine, ed. in charge, Richard M. Ketchum, author J.H. Plumb. American Heritage Publishing Co. Inc., New York, 1961.

Hutton, Edward, *Florence*. David McKay Co. Inc., New York, 1952.

Jameson, Anna, *Memoirs of Early Italian Painters, and of the Progress of Painting in Italy, Cimabue to Bassano*. John Murray, London, 1874.

Kronenberger, Louis, *Atlantic Brief Lives: A Biographical Companion to the Arts*. Little, Brown, Boston, 1971.

Lengyel, Alfonz, *The Quattrocento: A Study of the Principles of Art and a Chronological Biography of the Italian 1400s*. Kendall/Hunt Publishing Co., Dubuque, Iowa, 1971.

Lucas-Dubreton, J., *Daily Life in Florence in the Time of the Medici*. Translated from the French by A. Lytton Sells. Macmillan, New York, 1958.

Lucchesi, Venturino, and Bargellini, Simone, *Florence: An Illustrated Guide Book*. Saiga Paragon, Genoa.

Lucki, Emil, *History of the Renaissance--Economy and Society*. University of Utah Press, 1963.

Lumsden, Susan, *Prato's Art Patronage*. International Herald Tribune, May 22, 1987, pp. 7-8.

Marchini, Giuseppe, *Filippo Lippi*. Electa Editrice, Milan, 1975.

Mariani, Valerio, *Pittori protagonisti della crisi dell'400*. Libreria Scientifica Editrice, Naples, 1960.

von Martin, Alfred, *Sociology of the Renaissance*. Kegan Paul, Trench, Trubner & Co. Ltd., London, 1945.

Martines, Lauro, *The Social World of the Florentine Humanists*, 1390-1460. Princeton University Press, Princeton, New Jersey, 1963.

McCarthy, Mary, *The Stones of Florence and Venice Observed*. Penguin Books, Suffolk, 1982.

McGraw-Hill Encyclopedia of World Biography. Vol. 6, 1973.

Murray, Peter and Linda, *The Art of the Renaissance*. Thames and Hudson, London, 1963 (reprinted 1981).

Nigg, Walter, *Warriors of God, the Great Religious Orders and their Founders*. Edited and translated from German by Mary Ilford. Alfred A. Knopf, New York, 1959.

Oertel, Robert, *Fra Filippo Lippi*. Anton Schroll & Co., Vienna, 1942.

Olmert, Michael, *The New Look of the Brancacci Chapel discloses Miracles*. Smithsonian, Feb. 1990, pp. 94-103.

Pater, Walter, *The Renaissance--Studies in art and poetry*. 1893 text. University of California Press, Berkeley and L.A., 1980.

Patronage, Art and Society in Renaissance Italy. Edited by F.W. Kent and Patricia Simons. Clarendon Press, Oxford, 1987.

Pierotti-Cei, Lia, *Life in Italy during the Renaissance.* Translated by Peter J. Tallon, Minerva-Liber S.A., Milan, 1987.

Pittaluga, Mary, *Filippo Lippi.* Del Turco, Florence, 1948.

Portigliotti, Giuseppe, *Donne del Rinascimento.* Fratelli Treves Editori, Milan, 1930.

Powers, H. H., *The Art of Florence.* MacMillan, New York, 1931.

The Renaissance, Maker of Modern Man. National Geographic Society, Editorial consultant, Kenneth M. Setton. Washington, D.C., 1970.

Rowdon, Maurice, *Lorenzo the Magnificent.* Henry Regnery Co., Chicago, 1974.

Ruda, Jeffrey, *Filippo Lippi Studies.* Garland Publishing, New York-London, 1982.

di San Marzano, Betty, *Spoleto: Past and Present.* Spoleto, 1964.

The Society of Renaissance Florence, A Documentary Study. Edited by Gene Brucker. Harper & Row Inc., New York, 1971.

Steffensen, James L., *The Universal History of the World, Vol. VII--The Renaissance.* Golden Press, New York, 1966.

Stokes, Adrian, *The Quattro Cento: A Different Conception of the Italian Renaissance.* Schocken Books, New York, 1968.

Strutt, Edward C., *Fra Filippo Lippi.* George Bell & Sons, London, 1901. Reprinted AMS Press Inc., New York, 1972.

Supino, I.B., *Fra Filippo Lippi*. Fratelli Alinari Editore, Florence, 1902.

Van Vechten Brown, Alice, and Rankin, William, *Short History of Italian Painting*, and J.M. Dent & Sons Ltd., London, 1914.

Vasari, Giorgio, *Lives of the Artists*. A selection translated by George Bull. Penguin Books, Harmondsworth, Middlesex, 1965.

Vasari, Giorgio, *Vasari on Technique*. Translated by Louisa S. Maclehose. Dover Publications Inc., New York, 1960.

The Vespasiano Memoirs, translated by W.G. and Emily Waters, George Routledge & Sons Ltd., London, 1926.

Wackernagel, Martin, *The World of the Florentine Renaissance Artist*. Translated by Alison Luchs. Princeton University Press, Princeton, New Jersey, 1981.

Wherry, Albinia, *Stories of the Tuscan Artists*. J.M. Dent & Co., London, 1901.

Williamson, Hugh Ross, *Lorenzo the Magnificent*. G.P. Putnam's Sons, New York, 1974.

The World of Renaissance Florence. Edited by Giuseppe Martinelli. G.P. Putnam's Sons, New York, 1968.

BOOKS OF ITALIAN AMERICAN INTEREST

AMERICA'S ITALIAN FOUNDING FATHERS by Adolph Caso includes works by Beccaria and Mazzei. Cloth, ill., ISBN 0-8283-1640-4, $25.95.

DANCE OF THE TWELVE APOSTLES by P.J. Carisella reveals Italy's biggest sabotage of a German plan to destroy Rome. Cloth, ill., ISBN 0-8283-1935-9, $19.95.

DANTE IN THE 20TH CENTURY by Jorge Luis Borges et al includes articles by several American and European scholars on Dante. Cloth, ill., ISBN 0-9378-3216-2, $25.95.

FROGMEN--FIRST BATTLES by William Schofield and P. J. Carisella tell an authenticated story of the birth and deployment of underwater guerrilla warfare by the Italians of the World War II. Cloth, ill., ISBN 0-8283-1998-7, $19.95.

INFERNO by Dante Alighieri, translated by Nicholas Kilmer, illustrated by Benjamin Martinez, is rendered into modern English with a separate illustration for each canto. Cloth, ISBN 0-9378-3228-6, $19.50.

IMPERIAL GINA--The Very Un-Authorized Biography of Gina Lollobrigida by Luis Canales tells the story of this great Italian woman and actress. Cloth, ill., ISBN 0-8283-1932-4, $19.95.

ISSUES IN FOREIGN LANGUAGE AND BILINGUAL EDUCATION by Adolph Caso recounts the plight of the limited English-speaking students and their struggle to have the study of the Italian language introduced into our public schools. Paper, ISBN 0-8283-1721-6, $11.95.

ITALIAN CONVERSATION by Adele Gorjanc offers easy to follow lessons. Paper, ISBN 0-8283-1670-8, $11.95.

LIVES OF ITALIAN AMERICANS--They Too Made America Great by Adolph Caso contains 50 short biographies of those who contributed toward the formation of this nation. Cloth, ill., ISBN 0-8283-1699-6, $15.95.

MASS MEDIA VS. THE ITALIAN AMERICANS by Adolph Caso explores, critically, the image of the Italian Americans in the media. Paper, ill., ISBN 0-8283-1831-X, $11.95.

ODE TO AMERICA'S INDEPENDENCE by Vittorio Alfieri is the first such composition written on the emerging nation, in Italian with and English translation by Adolph Caso. Paper, ISBN 0-8283-1667-8, $11.95.

ON CRIMES AND PUNISHMENTS by Cesare Beccaria influenced Jefferson, Adams, Washington and many more. To a great degree, America owes its present form of government on this book. Introduction by Adolph Caso, paper, ISBN 0-8283-1800-X, $5.95.

ROGUE ANGEL--A Novel of Fra Filippo Lippi by Carol Damioli traces the tumultuous life of this Renaissance man who was both a great artist and womanizer. Cloth, ill., ISBN 0-9378-3233-2, $21.95.

TALES OF MADNESS by Luigi Pirandello, translated with an introduction by Giovanni Bussino, includes of the best of Pirandello's short stories dealing with the theme of human madness. Cloth, ISBN 0-9378-3226-X, $17.95.